THE WIFE ARRANGEMENT

USA TODAY *Bestselling Author*
PENNY WYLDER

ISBN-13: 978-1722652340

ISBN-10: 1722652349

CHAPTER ONE

Jasper

60 miles per hour.

70.

80.

85.

I floor the gas pedal, a wild grin on my face as I careen toward the corner of the track.

"Jasper…" warns a voice in my ear.

"I've got this," I murmur, in response to my usual test track monitor, safely above in a booth, watching me and this brand new gem of a car speed around the test track.

"We haven't tested the tires on curves yet.

Slow down to a more reasonable—"

I reach up and tap the headset attached to the crash helmet. The voice fades away. My smile widens.

The turn approaches. I swing the wheel hard. I feel the tires skid under the car, and for a pulse-stopping, heart-in-my-throat instant, I worry if the voice in my helmet was right. If I've taken the curve too fast, put too much stress on this new model, a car that hasn't even been unveiled to the public yet, let alone tested by the scientists and engineers who oversee the production of all new car regulations in the country.

If the car skids, flips, this could be it…

But then I feel the rubber screech, catch purchase again, and I rev the engine, accelerating with the turn instead of against it, so the car flows around the sharp turn of the track smooth as a knife through butter.

Safely onto the straightaway once more, I let out a loud *whoop* and gun it. I watch the speedometer leap up to 100, 120, 140... *Higher. Faster.*

I love this. I love getting to drive cars like this, and really put them through their paces. Drive them the way they're built to be driven—with abandon, and without road laws getting in the way. *Germany has it right*, I think briefly. If only the United States had its own autobahn. One road, one spot where people could let loose.

But, of course, that's a pipe dream for another time. For now, I'll have to settle for this closed test track, and the chance to pacify my inner speed demon from time to time—and earn a paycheck for it, no less.

I reach the makeshift finish line, really just a little dugout where we modify and prep the cars for the track, and squint through the visor of my crash helmet at my assistant, Greg.

Greg's enormous arms are crossed, his brow lowered in the thunderous expression he gets when he doesn't approve of something I've been doing. Of course, I'm *his* boss, so Greg can't really protest too much when I do things like this. But that doesn't mean he can't allow his disapproval to show on his face.

I skid to a halt outside the engineer shelter, and climb from the car while several test engineers flood the area, bending to take measurements of the axels, the tires, and one popping the hood to study how the engine held up, as another inspects the fuel gauges.

"How about that turning radius, huh?" I shout over the clank and clatter of tools and measuring devices. I sidestep a pair of engineers to reach Greg, and he removes his own earpiece.

"You shut off your radio," complains Greg, the voice in my ear, who has now become the constant voice in the back of my head. My conscience, one might even say. He's constantly watching me, overseeing things, warning me to slow down, take it easy, be more careful. I know my father puts him up to half of these disapproving glares and lectures, but even so, it can wear on a man. Especially when I know what I'm doing.

You might say I have a lot of practice

ignoring the conscience in the back of my head. "Your talking was distracting me," I say. "It was a finicky turn."

"Because you were driving at least twenty miles per hour faster than we'd run the car even in simulations," Greg mutters.

"And look how well it turned out!" I clap my assistant on the back. "Now we can all skip a few of the intermediate stress tests and put this model straight into pre-production status."

Greg rolls his eyes. "It was still an unnecessary risk—"

"But you say that about every risk," I point out, jamming a single finger into Greg's bicep. It barely makes a dent.

I take after my father's side of the family—all

lean, slim, sculpted muscle. We're built for running. Descended from the first marathon runners of ancient Greece, Dad always claims. Me, I mention that a fair amount too, albeit for different reasons. I blame those ancestors for my need for speed. "My speed demon was inherited," I always say. "Nothing I can do about it."

But Greg, he's a distant cousin, part of my dad's grandmother's vast clan. The line Greg comes from isn't built like marathoners so much as like walls.

Greg narrows his eyes at me.

I smirk and stride toward the main building. "Come on, worry wart. Lunch is on me to make up for your stress-induced high cholesterol levels."

"I would love to take you up on that, Jasper, but you have a lunch appointment." Greg flips open his tablet and squints down at the screen, scrolling through it with a finger.

"With who?" I frown. I don't remember any new clients planning to stop in and check out the factory today, and it's far too early in the production schedule for any fellow manufacturers to be poking around. Maybe early buyers? Wholesalers we invited to view the pre-public models...?

"Your father," Greg replies, and my stomach sinks. In an instant, the happy mood I manage to whip myself into on the test track evaporates, like a bubble popping in midair.

Not that my old man and I don't get along. Quite to the contrary. I work for him, I spend every day helping build the family business—testing our latest models of cars, suggesting improvements or modifications to the designs, marketing and selling them on the front end… I have a hand in every part of our company, and Dad's been grooming me to take over for him since I was about sixteen years old. I love this job, love my life, and I love my dad too. There's nothing I'd change about my life right now.

Well. Except for one tiny thing…

Dad's current mood. Because even without seeing his face, I can already guess what he's going to be on about today. The same thing he's been on about for the last several years. The same thing he railed at me over when I broke up with Karen, a friend-with-benefits who lasted a grand total of a month. The same thing he freaked out about again when I stopped seeing Meghan. Then Brooke. Then… who was that girl with the horses?

I can't even remember her name, truth be told.

What can I say? I've never been the dating type. Or the relationship type. Or the anything more than casual sex type. And who cares? Certainly not the girls I hook up with—I make it clear up front that things will only ever be casual between us, and none of them have complained. Well, except Stacey, who smashed the taillights of my car when I broke things off. But, well, you can see why I had to break off our casual arrangement, given her temper and possessive streak.

No, that one anomaly aside, nobody cares that I'm not the settling down type… Nobody except my father.

And with our family reunion looming on the

horizon, an enormous affair he hosts every five years, he has grandbabies on the mind worse than ever. This reunion will be the biggest of all, because at this reunion, Dad's announcing his retirement. His retirement and the appointment of the new company CEO. The future heir apparent to Quint Motors. *Me.*

But with all the reflecting Dad has been doing on the company's history, it just makes him more sentimental than ever about what's still missing in his life. Namely, grandchildren.

"I'm suddenly feeling really dizzy," I tell Greg. "Think I'm coming down with something. Head cold, maybe? Flu? Isn't it still flu season?"

Greg narrows his eyes at me. "Your father is already waiting out front in the Andromeda."

Ah, the Andromeda. The first car our

company, Quint Motors, ever released, way back in the 1970s when my dad was barely old enough to drive himself. He loves that thing. Not only because his father gifted it to him on his (way too young, if you ask me) wedding day. But also because it reminds him of family. If there's one thing that's more important to my father than our business, building cars, and putting the best product we can out into the market—it's the family behind all that.

"Family is the most important thing in the world," he's always saying. "Even when you want to strangle them." He usually adds that last line while he's glaring at me over a cup of coffee, having just learned from Greg (who, for being *my* personal assistant, can definitely be a real narc when it comes to sharing my extracurricular activities with the old man) about one of my exploits or another.

What can I say? It's my job to keep this family interesting.

I just wish it wasn't my job to listen to hours-long lectures on how interesting I make it. "No chance of talking my way out of this, huh?" I sigh and square my shoulders. "All right. Time to face the music."

"Bring a coat," Greg shouts at my retreating spine. "It's the Waldorf again."

Dad's favorite lunch spot. I'm halfway through the office when one of our other admins, an older man named Marco, waves a hand to flag my attention. "Jasper, thank goodness, I've been looking all over for you." He holds out a file almost as thick as my arm. "We got the list of interns for the summer

17

season. We need to start sorting them into departments…"

"Tell Greg to put something on my calendar," I say, already snatching a suit coat from the back of my chair and shrugging it on as I walk toward the distant front entrance, and the driveway where I can already see Dad's car idling. Tugging the jacket on over my work shirt at least gives the appearance that I dressed for the occasion.

So I think. Then I drop into the front seat, and find Dad eying my neck, nose scrunched up in disapproval.

"No tie?" he says. "And when was the last time you shaved?"

"This morning," I reply. "Not my fault I inherited your ridiculously fast hair-growth genes."

Permanent five o'clock shadow, just one of the many markers of a Quint man. That, a tall but muscular frame, and our thick dark hair—mine and Dad's look almost exactly the same, messy and wavy in front, with a shock falling across our eyes. Even though he's pushing sixty now, his is still as dark and thick as ever. Pretty sure Quint men will still pass for young men in their mid-twenties from behind right up until we're on our backs in coffins.

"Always blaming me." Dad shakes his head, but I notice he peels out of the driveway just as fast as always, and cuts corners the whole way to the Waldorf, speeding through every yellow light along the route.

My speed demon genes didn't pop out of thin air either, much as he never cares to admit where I got it.

We skid into the Waldorf parking lot, and Dad barely glances at the valet as he tosses his keys over his shoulder for the man to catch. I stride after him through the broad double doors, past the hotel lobby, and back into the dining room, where we've got our usual booth.

He's in a mood today. I can tell by the way he starts in before we've even had a chance to sit down, let alone give the menus a once-over. "The reunion is in one month, Jasper."

"Yes, I know. It would be impossible not to— it's all you've been talking about for the last six months." I shoot the waiter who's appeared at our table an apologetic glance, then wave him off to come back later.

"The reunion is in one month," Dad plows on as though I haven't even spoken, "and I'm planning to announce the company's future. My own retirement. My successor. But that's not what I'm really looking forward to. Do you know what I'm looking forward to most?"

Here we go. "What, Dad?" is all I say.

"The *family*. We'll get to see your cousin Sofia —you know she's pregnant again. That'll make five for her and her husband. And your cousin Alexander and his three little boys. Chloe and the twins; Luke and his newborn; and did I tell you Jason is married? I hear he and his wife are trying for a baby now, God bless them. I hope they don't have the same trouble your mother and I did."

"Dad…" Thankfully, the waiter returns to

spare me for the time being. I order a glass of water, but don't decide on any food for the time being. My stomach is already tensing up just listening to this.

Dad takes time to order his usual—steak, medium rare, a side salad and mashed potatoes, heavy on the gravy. He thinks it's healthier than French fries. Who am I to deny the old man one of his few vices in life?

Mom would be throwing a fit if she knew. She's always on about his cholesterol levels and the bad hearts that run in his side of the enormous family he's just been listing off.

The pause for food ordering only spares me for so long. Then Dad lays down his menu and crosses his hands on the table once more. "Your Aunt Zoe is a grandmother how many times over now?

Fifteen? Aunt Alyssa has Chloe's little twins to keep her busy. Uncle Xavier spoils Sofia's tribe rotten."

"Dad—"

"Everyone's family lines are carrying on except mine. Mine has stalled out like a bad clutch on a car destined for the junk yard."

I grimace. "Look, I'm not like my cousins, okay?"

"You mean you aren't a family man. More of a philandering man."

"Philandering implies it's not totally consensual on both sides." I roll my eyes. "And I never said I'm against starting a family—"

"Well clock's ticking, son, and you aren't getting any younger. Neither are your mother and I, for that matter."

"But I'm not going to throw myself into some crappy marriage with a wife I'm not that into just to satisfy you. Or anyone else, for that matter. It's my life, Dad."

"Your spoiled, easy life. Yes." Dad heaves a sigh. "Your mother is right. She tells me I spoiled you too much. Gave you too much. We were both so happy to have you, Jasper, after all that time and all that money and all that heartache spent trying. You have no idea what it was like. To watch my brother and sisters having children, yet be unable to conceive a child of my own. And your mother, her heartbreak every time we failed, I cannot even describe…"

And yet you continually try, I think. After all, he's told me this story—the saga of he and Mom trying to conceive me—about a hundred times. "Dad, I appreciate that you and Mom stuck with it. Honestly. But that's the thing—you had Mom. You were married. You knew you wanted a family with her. I'm…"

"Enjoying sleeping around too much to ever get serious about one woman or choose a wife? Yes, I've noticed." Dad glares at me over the top of his glass of water. "This is a family business, son. My grandfather founded Quint Motors, and then he passed the company on to my father before me. I'd planned to pass it on to you, son, after I go, so that one day, in the future, you can pass it on to your son or daughter next. But it's looking more and more like there won't be anyone for you to hand this company down to when the time comes."

I groan and lean back in my seat. "Dad, you're

being ridiculous."

"What do I always tell you is the most important thing?"

"Family, yes—"

"Even more important than money. Even more important than a successful business, or making good cars, or finding the right buyers. Family is all you have at the end of the day, when everything else fades. You say you know that, you claim to understand it, and yet here you are, no grandchildren, not even a decent prospect of a future wife to show for it. How can I believe that you really value family?"

"I put up with you every day, don't I?" I mutter.

Wrong direction to steer in. Dad's face goes white, then red-hot. "I've made this too easy for you.

I've let you waltz through business school and through the last ten years of working for us like you're the heir apparent. But this company would never have existed without family, and it won't exist without that support in the future." Dad leans forward and jams his finger into my face. "Plenty of your cousins would kill to be in your shoes. Given the real respect and family-mindedness they show, I have a mind to name one of them as the heir at the reunion."

"*What?*" I nearly shout. Other faces swivel in our direction, other people in the restaurant lean closer to spy. I ignore them, though I do lower my voice a touch. "That's insane, Dad. I've been involved in this business from the minute I was old enough to understand what a car was. I've devoted all my spare time to working for you, putting in the hours, understanding how every inch of this company operates."

"And yet you failed to understand the most important lesson—the most important *thing*—in the world."

"This is ridiculous. What does having a wife and kids have to do with owning a business?"

"Everything, son," Dad snaps. "That's what you don't see. That's what I won't wait around for you to wake up to."

"So, what? You're just going to sign Quint Motors over to my cousins, and that's it?"

"You could change my mind." Dad leans back in his seat. He eyes me now, cool once more, his expression composed.

Beneath the table, out of sight, I clench my fists. "How?" I ask through gritted teeth. I know I won't like whatever's coming next. But whatever I expect, it isn't this.

"Find a woman." He holds up a hand, forestalling my protest. Because it's not like I can't find women just about anywhere I go. "A *marriageable* woman," Dad clarifies. "A wife. If you can find a wife by the time we all leave for Greece, then maybe I'll believe you're as serious about this company's future —and more importantly, this *family's* future—as you claim to be."

"You sound like a crazy person. I'm not listening to this." I wave a hand to get the waiter's attention. I need the check. I'm out.

Dad lunges across the table and grabs my

wrist. "All your mother and I ever dreamed about was having a big family." His eyes bore into mine as he says it, as though he's willing me to understand.

But I don't. I don't get it. I've never felt the way about a woman like he felt about Mom. I've never looked at a girl and thought, *I'd like to have dozens of kids with her.* I'm just *not like him.* On some core level.

"You're our only shot at that now," Dad is saying. "You're our only hope at fulfilling our dream."

"Exactly." I stand, giving up on the waiter. "*Your* dream, Dad. That's what *you* wanted. I'm different, okay?"

"Well." Dad releases my wrist and turns his attention back to the table, unrolling his own silverware. Clearly he plans to stay and eat anyway. "If we're so different, then you won't care about my decision to hand the company over to one of your cousins instead. Maybe Alexander. He does always have good manufacturing suggestions..."

My blood boils. *Alexander is half the salesman I am,* I think. Last time we let him run a European business conference himself, he walked away without a single new buyer. *Not a single one.* You have to be completely incompetent to do that—Quint cars practically sell themselves.

"If you want to run this business into the ground, have at it," I mutter as I turn to stride away.

"One month," Dad calls at my retreating spine. "You have one month to prove to me you're not a lifelong bachelor after all, or I drop you from the company roster."

31

****

"I need a wife," I tell Greg.

Once he finishes laughing, I scowl and snatch the stack of intern applications from his hands.

"I'm serious," I say, fanning the pages of the applications, but not really paying any attention to the ink on the paper, what any of the words say. "Dad's talking about giving Alex the company if I don't get serious. Find someone to settle down with."

"*Alex*?" Greg says in the same tone you'd use about a pile of manure you stepped in. "The same Alex whose accountant we had to fire because he was embezzling thousands of dollars that Alex didn't even notice was missing?"

"One and the same." I drop the stack of intern applications once more with a groan. "Dad thinks Alex will be more serious about running the company because he's family-oriented. Him or any one of my other married-with-children cousins. He's holding it against me that I don't have a million grandkids for him to spoil yet." I run my hand through my hair, teeth gritted in frustration.

Over and over, ever since lunch, I've replayed our lunchtime fight in my head. And over and over, I just hear his voice on repeat. *If you can find a wife by the time we all leave for Greece...*

Crazy. He's crazy. That's a month away. And I'm not going to just marry some random woman to please him, to do what he says. It's my life. I get some damned say in it, don't I?

"He told me I had to be married by the reunion," I inform the ceiling. "Or he's giving Quint Motors to someone else in the family."

Greg laughs. Then he catches a glimpse of my expression, and sobers immediately. "But that's in a month. That's insane."

"I know." I roll my eyes once more.

Greg, on the other hand, gets a new expression. A tight-lipped one that I recognize.

His thinking face.

"Uh oh." I side-eye him. "You only ever look like that when you're about to suggest something completely batshit, you know."

"Because I think I am." Greg turns to face me. "You only need a wife for the reunion, right? Your father is stepping down, naming the new CEO at the retirement event they're all planning on day, what, four of the weeklong reunion?"

"Something like that," I agree.

"So you only need a wife for that long. Once he signs Quint Motors over to you, it doesn't matter what he wants—the company becomes yours."

I tilt my chair forward and tear my eyes from the ceiling, sensing where this is going. "Good thought, but unfortunately, it's not quite that cut-and-dry. Once he makes me CEO, Dad's still going to retain the majority share in the company stocks. Not to mention our family holds the rest of the stocks. He can bully and strong-arm them into ousting me the minute I ditch any temporary wife I show up with."

"True. Unless your father approves of the divorce," Greg says with a laugh, because my father,

Mr. Family Man's, favorite rant topic is about kids these days and how little they value lasting marriages.

But... "Hang on." Lightbulb. I look at Greg. "Say that again."

He frowns. "Unless your father approves of the divorce?" he repeats. "But, he never would, I mean, he doesn't approve of that unless..."

"Unless it's someone like the crazy cheating woman Luke left before his second wife?" I say, mind racing. "The one trying to get her hands on his inheritance. Or like the one Chloe split up with, the one she married when she was a teenager, he was a real trip, utterly classless..."

Greg sits forward in the chair, following my drift. "So if you do find a wife, but she's absolutely completely awful..."

"Then Dad would be begging me to divorce her. He'd be completely apologetic for forcing me into marrying so quickly in the first place too. And I can tell him I'll only divorce her if he makes me CEO without any of his crazy conditions."

"That could work," Greg agrees. "But where the hell are you going to find a woman like that? Just start scouring local bars for a pick-up?"

He keeps talking, but I don't hear the rest. My eyes have landed on a cast-aside stack of papers, and my brain is already ticking into overtime. I reach out and snatch up the pile of intern assignments once more. "It has to be someone desperate," I hear myself saying. "Not an ounce of class in her. Someone who doesn't fit in our world, someone who'll take to rich like a fish out of water. The most untrustworthy gold-digger type you can find."

Greg slides the stack of intern files out of my hands then. "In that case," he says, flipping through it with the practiced eye of a man who's already read through this file at least a dozen times today. "I have the perfect candidate in mind…"

With that, he withdraws a single slip of paper with my one last chance at freedom written on it.

"Deeandra Smith," I read aloud.

CHAPTER TWO

Dee

"Holy shit, Melissa, you are *not going to believe* where I'm headed right now," I shout into my car phone speaker.

"Walmart," my best friend guesses.

Bless her heart. "I said you wouldn't believe it, not that it's the most believable place I could be at noon on a Tuesday." I roll my eyes.

"Just trying to be realistic, Dee." In the background, I hear the fuzz of the TV, and the distant shouts of children. Melissa watches her neighbor's brood of four kids on weekdays to earn extra cash because her husband Arnold can barely afford their rent, even working double overtime shifts down at the plant.

"I told you, I don't need the greeter job anymore. I'm moving up in the world."

"Yeah, moving up to where, exactly?" Then Melissa shouts something else, which sounds like a string of curse words followed by a yell at one of the kids.

I wince in sympathy and wait for the havoc to die down on her end. "I got an internship!"

"Oh awesome! Congratulations!" Melissa returns to the phone breathing harder than before, but I've learned by now not to ask for more details. It'll likely involve an excess of diapers, puke stains, or worse. "I hope it's not one of those unpaid ones

where they work you to the bone for zero salary..."
Her voice goes hesitant again.

Melissa knows how hard I worked to get my degree in a correspondence course, so that I could start applying for real jobs. Tear myself away from the minimum wage retail industry that ate the rest of my family—what little remained, anyway—alive. "It's paid," I reassure her, my tone cheerful. "And better than I was making, too."

"Well praise for that. Then again, just about anything would be better paid than a package store greeter." Melissa grunts, and I hear a toddler squeal somewhere near the receiver. "I keep telling you, you should get into the nannying gig, it's decent money."

"I think it takes a real saint like you to put up with *other* people's kids for so long." I laugh.

"What, don't you want a whole passel of your own?" I hear more grunts, and then the toddler near the phone begins to yell something about a bottle.

"Sure, eventually," I shout back, over the sound of wails. "But with the right person, you know? Not just like… Stealing my neighbor's kids."

Melissa bursts into laughter. "Hey, don't knock it till you try it. And *you*, Ryan, *knock it off.*" She vanishes for a few moments, then returns once more, torn between laughter and an exhausted-sounding resignation. "So, where is this mystery gig, huh?"

"That's the best part…" I grin to myself and pause for dramatic effect. "Quint Motors."

"What?! No way!" Now Melissa sounds like the screechy one. "That's amazing—you've been geeking out over their cars for, what, the past decade?

Ever since Will took you to prom in his old vintage…
what was it called?"

"Andromeda."

"That's right. The one that looks like it fell
straight out of the sixties version of a sci-fi movie."

I roll my eyes, but also grin as I check my
directions and make a right turn through a packed
intersection. "It's a classic. As are most of the models
they've put out ever since. Not to mention word on
the street is that their forthcoming model is going to
blow the luxury car market wide open."

"God, can you imagine?" For a moment, I
hear Melissa pause on the other end. "Having enough
money to waste on cars like that?"

"I can." I sigh under my breath. I *have* been
imagining it, for just about all my life. But for a girl

43

like me, owning a car like the ones Quint Motors produces is a pipe dream. Still, working for them, and with those cars, could be the next best thing. Right?

"Oh right, I forget that you like that kind of stuff. If you were rich, you'd be insufferable, wouldn't you? Buying some new fancy car every other week, speeding them so fast down roads you flip them into telephone poles…"

I gasp in faux offense. "When I own my private fleet of Quint Motors cars, I will *never* crash them into something so quaint as a telephone pole."

"Only the most expensive car crashes for you?" Melissa laughs. "But seriously though, congrats again. That's, like, the perfect job for you. Miss Wannabe Mechanic. Do you get to wear jeans and greasy shirts to work too? If they try to make you dress up like an office girl, I think you might explode," she warns.

I snort. "I own dresses!" I protest.

"One dress."

"Okay, one dress. It must have worked well in my preliminary interview because they gave me the internship, right?"

"Uh huh. And what are you wearing today? Same dress?"

Crap. I glance down at myself. The plain blue shift-dress seemed about right for my first day of interning. It's office-y, boring. Everything I normally hate. But I scored this one on megasale for five bucks, and it's served me well in situations like this. When I have to, on occasion, I clean up nice. "Do you think they'll notice?" I ask.

"Who interviewed you, the same people you'll be working with?"

"No, some assistant. Greg something?"

"Hmm. If it's a guy, he might not notice." A pause. "Unless he's gay."

"Hmm." I think back to the interview. "Really couldn't tell."

"Then you might get caught. But hey, who cares, it's just one day. Pretend you're doing laundry if someone asks about the same outfit thing. Or, ooh, do you have a scarf or something in the car? Toss that on, change up the look a little."

My head swims. *Dammit.* I didn't even think about this stuff. I'm used to rolling into work in my only pair of non-completely-holy jeans and my assigned uniform polo top. Not having a whole closet full of appropriate clothing to choose from. "Thanks, Melissa."

"What are friends for?" She laughs. "In this case, whipping your tomboy butt into shape. Okay, I gotta run—oh God, Simon, no!" The other end of the phone dissolves into screams and distant peels of triumphant toddler laughter.

I disconnect, just in time it seems, as I pull into the Quint Motors parking lot. Now my face really does flush, not from the idea of wearing the wrong dress, though. Because arriving to *this* parking lot in my junky, beat-up, twenty-year-old car—the one I've just barely been able to keep wheezing along through life with a lot of TLC and a really good friend down at my local mechanic who slips me spare parts for wholesale price when nobody's looking—is

47

way more embarrassing than being caught in a cheap work outfit.

I slide into a free spot between a 2018 Phoenix and a 2019 Aspen. I didn't even know the new Aspen was *out* yet. Maybe that's some big-wig's car who got it on pre-sale. I eyeball it with interest as I open my car door, grab my purse, and square my shoulders. Right. Time to do this. Time to change my life from boring-minimum-wage-retail-worker to Girl With Real Job.

All I need to do is ace this internship and land a permanent spot with the company. How hard could that be?

This is what I've worked for.

Growing up, Ma always told me that if you put your noses to the grindstone, you'd be rewarded in spades. Never stop working, she'd always say, and eventually you'll make it. The tortoise and the hare was her favorite parable, you might say.

This is for you, Ma, I think, a little pang in my heart at that. I wish she could be here to see it all finally pay off—all these years of hard work. But unfortunately, cancer claimed her far too young. It left me solo, considering my father had died just a few years before her, and my older brother ran off the minute he died. I was a wreck when she first passed, but now, with a few years' space, the pain has gotten manageable. That, and I have Melissa, and our little tight-knit circle of friends to serve as my new family.

But there's still an ache. Still a little family-shaped hole in my chest where my old life used to be.

I push that thought to the back of my mind

and wipe the frown off my face. Today is a happy day. Not a day to cry over the past—a day to look to the future, to the bright new life I'm going to build. One that would make Ma proud. One that *will* make her proud, from wherever she is looking down on me now.

My smile returns with a vengeance and I slam my car door and stride into the lobby of Quint Motors with my head held high, chin up. Whatever this new internship entails—which, from the job description on the application site sounded like a little bit of everything, with some hands-on experience with the cars, some office training, even the potential for a day on the test track with new models (I definitely geeked out over that last possibility)—I'm going to ace it.

"Hi," I tell the receptionist. "I'm here for the intern program?"

The receptionist doesn't answer at first. She's too busy staring off at the far corner of the lobby. I follow her gaze, turning to see two men in deep conversation. One, the older one, looks vaguely familiar. The younger one looks angry, and a lot like the older man, and also... well. I can tell why the receptionist is distracted. Because damn, that man is built.

He has to be, what, 6'4", 6'5"? And all lean muscle, too. Not body-builder huge, but the sort of guy who could unexpectedly lift you single-handedly and drag you in a fireman's carry to the nearest bed. With those sharp biceps of his, the cut jawline and razor cheekbones over his perfect bow lips, I could imagine a thing or two to do in bed with him.

Just then, as though sensing my gaze—or maybe the receptionist's—he turns. I catch a glimpse of dark, sharp eyes. The kind of eyes that could pin you in place with one glance, while he went to work spreading your legs open, bending you over a desk...

My cheeks go hot, and I whip around. Somewhere behind me, I catch a distant shout, and then a door slams. Only then does the receptionist tear her eyes away, back to me. She smiles once, apologetically.

"Just spying on the family drama," she says with a laugh and a little flutter of a sigh that doesn't convince me. *Sure*. Drama. That's why you were eying Mr. Hunky over there like a fresh cut of steak. "That's Mr. Quint and his son, Jasper," she clarifies, in response to my blank stare.

Oh. My eyes widen. That's why the older man looked familiar. Antoine Quint—I've seen his photo in about a thousand magazines, usually in those Magnate of the Year type features, but occasionally in the Rich Older Men (And Their Hot Wives) type categories too.

With a father like that, and a mother like the bombshell I've seen pictured on Antoine's arm at red carpet photo shoots, it's no wonder his son—Jasper, was it?—is so distracting to the poor receptionists around here.

"What did you need, again?" the receptionist is staring at me.

I flush once more. "Oh. Ah. Internship. I'm here for. I mean, that's me." Damn. Now I've gone and caught fluster from ogling the owner's son. I clear

my throat. "Could you point me toward where the

new interns should head?"

Now it's the receptionist's turn to give me a

sarcastic, knowing smirk. "Sure thing. Let me just get

you checked in." She taps on her computer keyboard.

"Name?"

"Dee Smith."

She hums under her breath to herself, and

then a little puzzled crease appears on her forehead.

"I see a Deeandra Smith?"

My blush, if possible, worsens. "Ah, yes.

That's my legal name. Would it be possible to change

it to Dee in the system? I sort of hate the full thing."

"It is pretty bad," she agrees with a laugh,

which only makes my body feel hotter. More out of

place.

"My father's suggestion," I say, because for some reason, suddenly, I feel the need to defend my mother. To who? To this random receptionist? I clear my throat. "Anyway. Thanks for that. Um, where do I go?"

"Straight down the hall on your right. Greg Park's office."

"Oh." My forehead creases. "I thought orientation would be with the whole group of us?" I've been in Greg's office—it's where I interviewed, my first and only time in this building, almost a month ago now. And I'd heard there were three or four dozen other interns starting the program at the same time.

"It will be," she says, "But Greg put a flag in

the system and asked me to send you to his office first."

"Oh." My stomach flips over. Suddenly, my excitement is turning into something more painful. Bees stinging at my innards in panic. "Is everything all right?" *I can't lose this job. Not before I've even started it.*

"I'm sure it's fine." She offers me a big smile, and then turns to greet someone behind me. "Hi, checking in?" When I don't move, she flashes me another smile, more pointed this time. "You're free to go ahead, Deeandra."

Great. So I managed to piss off the receptionist already, and I've only been inside the building for about five minutes. "Thanks so much," I call over my shoulder, striding away with one last pained look at the new girl who just entered, another intern, who's not being directed to the interviewer's private office before what was supposed to be our orientation.

My stomach sinks further.

Keep it together, Dee. This will be fine. I'm sure it's just about some little thing, maybe paperwork I forgot to send in.

I reach Greg's door and knock lightly. The door is open a crack, but I don't want to just go barging straight in. After a moment, a voice inside the office clears his throat. "Come in."

I suck in a deep breath, pray to anyone up there who might be listening, and shove the door open to step inside. Just like last time, I have to carefully squeeze in between the one visitor's chair and the door. Unlike last time, there are heaps more paperwork spilling across the desk. Behind said desk, Greg looks a lot more haggard than the last time I saw him. He has huge bags under his eyes, and his hair is a mess—not the cute on-purpose messy, either.

"Hi," I say with a bright smile. "Is everything all right? I'm Dee," I add, when he stares at me in confusion. "Front desk said to stop here before orientation."

"Dee, Dee… Oh, Deeandra!" His face brightens. He lifts one of the stacks of paper and slides something out from beneath. This very nearly causes an avalanche, and I leap forward to grab the topmost stack for him, and hold it in place while he slides the file out.

On the front of the file, I spot my own name in big block letters.

I force myself to keep breathing, taking deep, slow breaths, as I lower myself into the chair across from him. *This will be fine,* I reassure myself. *It's nothing.*

"So. Dee, is it?" Greg smiles at me, a little less flustered now. Then he laughs. "That's right, you told me this in the interview. I'm sorry, I've been such a space cadet. I remember you now." His gaze drops to my dress, and his head tilts to one side. For a second, he looks almost calculating.

Damn. Does he recognize this dress, too?

I swallow around a lump in my throat. "So, you wanted to talk to me?"

"Yes. I was looking over your résumé, and I just had a couple of questions I wanted to clarify, if you don't mind."

"Of course not." *Smile, Dee. Smile through the*

panic. "Fire away," I say, and follow it up with an awkwardly loud laugh. Did I mention I'm great at lying?

"Where did you go to school again?"

"Gerold College. It's um, it's an online college —I only got an associate's, it should say on there…"

"Yes, it does." He tilts his head to peer up at me. "Aced all your courses, though. Why didn't you go for a higher degree? Seems like you're smart."

My cheeks flush. I'm going to turn into a tomato at this rate. "Uh… I couldn't really… afford it," I finish the sentence in a mumble. "But I'm planning on going back. As soon as I get enough credits—which is where I figured this internship would come in handy. I want to get a BA in business, see, and with an associate's and some experience under my wing, I might be able to—"

"Where did you grow up?" he speaks over me.

"Oh, right around here." I perk up at this
easier question. "Down on Mercy Street, near St.
Martha's."

He frowns. I realize I've put my foot in it
again. Because, of course, a guy like *him*, working for
a company like *this*, hears St. Martha's, and all he
thinks is... "You mean by the squats?"

"It's not... I mean, okay, it used to be a pretty
bad area. But it's gotten a lot better in recent years.
And, I mean, the community itself is really great,
really supportive—"

"Dee," he says.

I snap my mouth shut. *Here it comes.* He's
going to fire me. Tell me thanks but no thanks, you

61

aren't who I thought you were. You of the used dress and the associate's degree where everyone else has a BA. You, girl from the wrong side of the tracks, who thinks she can flounce over here into the real world unopposed.

I ball my fists, dig my nails into my palms to prepare myself for it.

But, "This isn't an interrogation," is all he says, and I blink in surprise.

"Sorry, I guess I'm just confused…" I press my lips together. "We already interviewed, so I thought we'd covered all this, what is—"

"This internship isn't what you think," he interrupts. "At least, not for you. We reviewed your application, my boss and I together, and we'd like to give you a special assignment. If you're amenable to it, of course."

"Of course," I say. "Anything you need."

"It's not me so much as my boss. He needs…
Ah. Well. He needs a woman to pretend to be his
wife."

I stiffen. Blink. Stare across the desk at Greg
in shock. It takes a few moments for the words to
sink in.

Once they do, the anger hits. I surge to my
feet. "I don't know what kind of person you think I
am, but—"

"I know it's extremely unusual, please wait,"
Greg shouts when I reach for the door. "Just hear me
out. My boss, Jasper Quint, he's the son of the
owner."

I hesitate, one hand on the doorknob. *Jasper.*

The man I saw in the lobby earlier. The sexy, ripped one distracting the poor receptionist. "What the hell does *he* need a pretend wife for?" I hear myself saying before I can think better of it.

Greg bursts into laughter. "I take it you've seen him, then." He smirks. "Look, Ms. Smith, it's very simple. Mr. Quint—senior, I mean—is a family man. He's pressuring Jasper to get married. Jasper needs a woman to come along to a family event, big reunion happening next month. Just wear a ring, pretend you eloped, and meet the family. As soon as the vacation is over, you can come back here and end the charade. Go back to living your life. *With*," Greg adds, with another glance at my résumé, "this fantastic internship on your résumé and a handwritten letter of recommendation for the university of your choosing from Jasper himself. Plus, naturally, the payments we already agreed upon. And we could throw in a bonus at the end, for sticking out the whole vacation."

"A bonus," I hear myself saying, "for going on vacation to Greece and pretending I've married a car magnate." My voice sounds flat. Shocked.

This can't be happening.

Then again...

"Ms. Smith, I should remind you that the alums of our internship program have a near 99% placement rate in car design programs throughout the country. Most place into top schools, too—and that's without a personal recommendation from the soon-to-be new CEO."

My eyes widen. "Jasper is taking over?" There

have been rumors for years, yet nothing confirmed.

"That's… a little bit what all this mess is about." Greg sighs. "I know this all sounds crazy. But trust me, if you knew this family as well I do, it makes perfect sense. For them, anyway." Greg offers a little laugh.

I drift away from the door, back toward my seat. "It sounds like I'd have to get to know this family as well as you, if I took on this job. Vacationing with them in Greece? At a reunion?"

"They only do that once every 5 years. Return to the homeland to celebrate where it all began, about six generations ago now." Greg smirks. "It's definitely an eventful week, most times. Always some new addition to the family to greet, old grudges and dramas that surface… If nothing else, I can promise you'd have an eventful time posing as Jasper's better half."

Emotions war inside me. On the one hand, this sounds… well, like Greg put it, crazy. And I'm looking for job experience; help with my BA degree, not my Mrs. Degree.

But on the other hand, as roundabout as it seems, this *would* apparently get me a strong letter of recommendation toward said degree. Not to mention the pay is already pretty nice, and Greg mentioned a bonus if I wind up completing the whole reunion. "When you say bonus…" I start to reply.

Just then, the doorknob to the office turns, and the door swings inward, smacking the side of my chair in the cramped space. "Greg, I need the numbers from yesterday's stress test to run down to engineering—oh." Jasper Quint stops dead in the doorway, eyes locked on me.

Fuck. He's even hotter up close than he was across the entrance lobby. This close to him, I can appreciate the sharpness of his cheekbones, the hard planes of his angular face. A face currently scrunched up in displeasure.

"I apologize," Jasper says, tearing his gaze from me to glance at Greg instead. "I didn't know you were in the middle of something."

"Actually, in the middle of finding the perfect candidate for your little, ah… side venture." Greg darts a glance at the door.

Jasper stares at me with new eyes, this time. If anything, he looks more offended than before. "Oh. I see." He steps inside fully and shuts the door after him. Then he leans back against it, arms crossed in a way that makes his biceps bulge. My eyes dart immediately to the plane of his stomach, visible beneath the tight black T-shirt he's wearing. A shirt that only accentuates the sharp lines of his abs. "So you're wife material, huh?"

My cheeks flush. "Well, I don't know about that…" I babble, and that only makes me blush worse. "I mean, I… Greg was just explaining what you're looking for. I was…"

"We were just discussing bonus options, actually. A completion bonus if she survives the full reunion week with all of your relatives in tow." Greg flashes Jasper a meaningful smile.

"Right. Bonus. Yes." Jasper, meanwhile, doesn't drag his eyes from mine. "So you're in this for the money, then?"

"No," I blurt, then realize how that sounds. "I'm in it for the recommendation letter, actually. Sir." I don't know why I added the sir. I curse myself mentally. Normally I'm better than this at talking to guys. I'm most guys' best friend. The girl they love to talk to, pour their hearts out to. The girl whose shoulder they cry on while they're pining for some other girl. "It's a pretty unusual situation, you have to admit," I say, to cover up my weird formality. "I came here expecting to get valuable job experience. To be able to actually work with the cars your family produces."

His eyebrows rise at that. "You're actually interested in the cars? I thought all our interns just came for the pay grade and the letters of recommendation in engineering schools."

"Those too," I say with a smirk. "But yeah, I'm really in it for the cars. I love all the company's designs. Been a huge fan ever since I first rode in an Andromeda."

"Which year?" Jasper quirks a brow.

"Oh, the '78. No offense, but I tried the '82 too, and it just—"

"Doesn't have the same smooth ride, I agree." He's smiling now. Then he seems to catch himself, and his expression snaps back into serious mode. "So. You're interested in the position, Ms. …?"

"Dee," I say. I rise and smooth down my skirt, then offer a hand. "If we're going to pose as lovers, you'd better know my first name."

He takes my hand. The moment our skin

brushes, an electric shock shoots through me, all the way to my toes. Then he lets go, far too fast, and I'm left trying to catch my breath. "Well, Dee." His gaze drips over my body, and for a second, I feel hot all over, watching him check me out. Then he shrugs and glances at Greg. "I could do worse."

My stomach drops. "Excuse me?"

He turns back to me with a smirk. "Just an observation."

This is going to be a harder assignment than I thought. "How long did you say this would take, again?" I say, turning to face Greg instead of this jerk.

Greg looks like he's struggling to maintain a straight face. "The reunion is one month away, Ms. Smith."

A month. A month of this, then a week of

Jasper's apparently even crazier family. "I'll see if I can stomach feigning an interest in him for that long." I shoot Jasper a sideways glare.

He just grins wider. "On second thought, this might be more fun than I thought."

"So can I take that as a yes?" Greg calls loudly, interrupting his boss's banter. I have a feeling Greg wants Jasper to shut up almost as much as I do right now.

He was so damned attractive when he wasn't talking...

Still, despite the annoying comments, I feel myself nodding. I need that recommendation letter. Not to mention the cash. It'll help pay my way through the university I plan to apply to with that letter.

"Great." Greg claps his hands together, so loud that both Jasper and I startle. We'd taken to glaring sidelong at one another in the interim. "I'll draw up a contract for you to sign, Ms. Smith. Oh, and, ah…" He glances at the clock behind him. "You don't need to bother with the intern orientation today. In fact, I think it would be better if we didn't have you on the premises, in case Mr. Quint Sr. stops by anywhere…"

My face must have fallen, because Jasper suddenly pipes up. "Nonsense. The more face-time my future fiancée has with my father, the better. But I agree, we'll skip the boring orientation." His eyes dart to mine again. He's smiling once more, a little grin that plays at the edges of his mouth. Damn him. He's enjoying this. Teasing me. "You said you like our cars.

Come on a tour with me, Dee, and we can get to know each another."

He holds up an arm. For a moment, I stare at it like it's a snake about to bite me.

But Jasper just tilts his head, smirking. "You'll need to work on your acting skills if you want to fool my family into thinking we're together. Come on, I don't bite…"

Reluctantly, I slide my arm through his.

As he tightens his grip on my arm, pinning it against his side, which I can't help but notice is warm and all kinds of muscular, he adds one final comment under his breath. "Well, not often, anyway."

My face flushes. Standing this close, his scent washes over me, warm and heady. Something strong, masculine, almost piney maybe. I can't place it, yet it seems vaguely familiar. I'm still distracted by that when Greg opens the office door for us.

"See you later, future Mrs. Quint." He flashes me a wink, and with that, I'm dragged off into my accidental future.

CHAPTER THREE

Dee

"This is the show room." Jasper flicks on an overhead light. Suddenly, a room filled with more luxury cars than I've ever seen in my life explodes into view. My jaw drops.

There must be at least 200 million dollars' worth of vehicles in this one room alone.

We're on the lower level now, beneath the manufacturing plant we just toured, and the artists' design rooms above that. My arm is still looped through Jasper's, in case anyone stumbles across us on this tour and sees us. But I have to admit, as we've paced through the building, I've gotten more and more used to having his arm against mine, his muscles brushing my arm with every step we take, and the warm, heady scent of him filling my senses. Flooding me, overwhelming me.

"We don't use it much anymore," he's saying. "Most buyers come to one of our storefront locations to check out the merchandise. But occasionally we get wholesale buyers looking for a tour, or some of our more elite customers, the ones who don't wish to be seen anywhere public."

"Like who?" I ask, though truth be told, I'm more interested in the cars themselves. I spot an '88 Phoenix, a brand new Vine, a couple Cougars that would give race car drivers a run for their money, given how the engines are built.

"Couldn't say. It'd be breaking the sacred auto customer-seller code."

I shoot him a side-eye. "What are you, a doctor now?"

"We provide a service. An important one. We're giving people dreams, here."

I snort with laughter. Though as we pass the latest Cougar, I run a hand along the bright cherry red finish of its hood. "Dreams of modded V-8 Dynamo engines?" I say, still smirking. "Or just dreams of being the boy in the yard—or on the racetrack in this case—with the newest and coolest toy?"

Jasper tilts his head to one side. Whenever he does that, a shock of his dark hair falls across one eyebrow, and makes him look way too damn distracting for his own good. "A little bit of both," he says, studying me.

My cheeks flush, and I look away. "What?" I snap.

He shrugs. The movement makes his arm brush mine again, tantalizingly distracting. "You just surprise me, that's all," he says. "I didn't think you really knew your stuff."

I bristle. "I told you I'm here for the cars."

"Right, right. Not the wedding bells. Message received. Still, I've never met a girl who could actually talk shop the way you do."

"No other women work here?" I side-eye him, voice laced with sarcasm.

"Okay, point. But most of the other women working here who I've spoken to have been far more interested in... well, getting under *my* hood than under any vehicle's."

I roll my eyes. "Maybe you should try talking to the girls who aren't drooling over you, then. It could be healthy for you. Having females in your life who don't fawn over everything you do."

"People don't fawn over me," he protests. "They just show an adequate level of appreciation for what I bring to the table."

"What, a hot body and not much else?" I mean it to be an insult. Instead, he grins.

"So you do think I'm hot."

"I never…" I groan. "That's not what I meant. Don't you care about the non-superficial stuff?"

"Like my shiny race cars?" He laughs. "Of course I do. I also care about making money from

81

those shiny race cars, and producing good products so that other people will also appreciate our shiny race cars. I'm not the shallow monster you seem to think I am."

"You aren't exactly convincing me otherwise." I don't know when it happened, but we've stopped walking now. We're face-to-face, and I stare up at him, breath catching in my throat at his sudden proximity. He's staring down at me, searching, those dark eyes boring into mine as he looks for… what, exactly? An apology? I won't give him one. I square my shoulders.

The motion seems to distract him. Tear his mind back to the present moment. He shakes his head and steps away, gesturing to me. "Let's go for a drive."

In spite of myself, my heart skips. "Really?"

"I'll even let you have the wheel. You claim to be such a car lover. Let's see how well you drive on a test track."

My jaw drops. This day just keeps getting stranger and stranger. Swinging back and forth from crazy propositions to annoying new bosses I'm supposed to pretend to be marrying, to my dream event suddenly crashing in my lap. I've always wanted to drive a race car on a closed test track. To really find out how fast I can go, and how hard I can push a car.

"You mean it?"

"God, you look like Christmas just came early." He laughs. "I've never met anyone as hot for cars as I am." He tilts his head, considering me. "All right, little Ms. Smith. Let's put you through the paces, and see how well you can handle a real stick shift." He smirks, inviting a comment, but I don't take the bait.

I'll show you how well, I think. And now it's my turn to be the one smirking.

****

I floor the gas pedal. We fly toward the distant side of the track, and my heart pounds in my ears, my heart leaping into my throat.

I feel... *alive.*

"Whoa there," Jasper says from the passenger side of the car, but there's laughter in his tone. "You're almost as reckless as me."

"Almost?" I counter, a single eyebrow raised, as the first turn approaches. Then I cut the wheel hard and skid into the turn. For a second, the tires slide under us—holy shit. I'm actually drifting. I've never been able to drive fast enough to try this move before, and I've always wanted to. I let out a shout of sheer joy, and hear Jasper joining me.

Then we skid a little too far, and I grab for the gear shift, scrambling to get us back under control. For a second, Jasper's hand closes around mine on the shift. He locks eyes with me, and gears it into a lower gear, at the exact same instant that I hit the clutch. We transition together, smooth as ice, and then I'm back on the straightaway, and he lets go of my hand, and leaves behind a rush of tingles all along my arm.

Half a minute later, I pull up to the finish line, beaming like an idiot, and spin to face him. "So? Am I as reckless as you or more?" I ask, grinning.

But Jasper's expression has shifted from

lighthearted to something serious, penetrating. "I'm tempted to say more," he replies, voice low and husky, "But quite frankly, I didn't think that was possible."

He's looking at me like he's never seen anything like me before. Like I'm suddenly, unexpectedly, the most fascinating person in the room. And then he's leaning closer, and I find myself mirroring him, unable to tear my eyes from his, those dark, deep pools that latch onto me, seem to peer straight through me into my soul.

"Where the hell did you learn to drive like that?" he asks, eyebrows lifted.

"Oh, you know." I shrug one shoulder, try for a smile. "Grew up racing my dad out in the back country roads by our old farm." *Where did that come from?* I haven't thought about those days in years. I'm not sure I ever even put together the connection between my love of cars and those distant memories, me a little ten-year-old with legs too short to even reach the pedals, and Dad strapping some pedal extenders he jerry-rigged onto his old Jeep so I could reach enough to bump over the dirt paths to the fields he used to keep.

We moved away from the farm when he got sick, headed into the city, where we stayed after he died. My chest aches with the memory.

But Jasper is right here with me, reaching up to tuck a stray hair behind my ear, his gaze intent on mine. "So you were close with your family?"

"Oh, yeah. Family means everything," I reply without thinking about it.

Jasper's hand lingers on my cheek, hot against

my skin. My eyes are back on his again. He grins, and finally drops his hand, turning to face front. "Do you want to go again?"

My face, still flushed red from his touch, and the close encounter, lights up. "Oh hell yes."

He laughs. "Have at it."

I speed us through another three loops around the track, until my hands are shaking from the adrenaline rush, and my head swims with the high. There really is nothing like this—flying over the pavement at death-defying speeds, all the while knowing that I'm in complete control. At the end of my race, I decide to go for the full drift. I spin the car wheel and hit it at just the right angle to send the car lurching around a corner at a breakneck speed. It throws us both to the side of our seats, and I white-knuckle the wheel to hold on. When we finally level out on the straight again, both of us are cheering in unison, and I spin to face Jasper, laughing, unable to believe how well that worked, how good it felt.

And then his hands are cupping my face, pulling me to him, and our mouths collide.

At first, all I taste is spearmint. Then I part my lips, let his tongue slip through mine and wrestle with mine, and I sink forward, into the kiss, losing myself in his scent—dark and heady, like a drug I could never get enough of—and the way he tastes, like salt and sweet and something I can't resist.

Then I remember who I am. Who *he* is, and what we've agreed to do.

I jerk back, breath coming hard and fast, and lean away from him, despite every muscle in my body crying out in protest. "We can't do that," I say, before I even realize I agreed to let my mouth speak.

"Why not?" he asks. His dark eyes are still fixed on mine, unreadable. But there's passion in that gaze, a white-hot desire that I can feel mirrored in my own. His heart must be beating every bit as fast as mine, thundering with all that adrenaline.

That's all it is, I tell myself. The adrenaline, making me reckless, foolhardy. "I just met you," I say, turning away from him, tearing my eyes off his, to start the car back into motion and roll slowly toward the pull-off where I can park it. "And besides, I agreed to be your *fake* wife, not a real one."

"Nothing wrong with having a little fun along the way," he points out. "Besides, it would help sell the story."

"Oh, so you just kissed me to sell the story to this whole bunch of witnesses?" I wave at the empty track with one hand, and with the other, steer the car into the parking area.

"You know what I mean. It's good to test out our chemistry. Make sure that will play well in front of others."

I roll my eyes. "You're impossible."

"Impossible to resist?" When I cast another glance at him, he's grinning, a knowing smirk on those full lips of his. Almost like he knows how much I enjoyed that damn kiss. Almost like he knows I'm already picturing doing it again, but for longer—crawling over into the passenger side of the car and tearing his shirt off, and running my hands over those sculpted abs of his, which I can already see through

91

that damn tight T-shirt fabric…

"Oh please." I roll my eyes. "Are you always this overconfident?"

"I wouldn't call it overconfident. Just the correct amount of confidence. For example, I'm *confident* you enjoyed that kiss just now as much as I did."

"I… That's…" I sputter, then shake my head. "That's hardly the point." I shove the car into park and push the door open. "We work together, Jasper. Whether your coworkers know the exact terms of our business arrangement or not, it's important to me to keep this professional. Understand?"

"Understood." His eyes lock on mine for a moment before I climb out of the car. "But you didn't deny it, I'd like to point out," he adds.

I groan. "Are we done with this portion of the tour?"

"We're done," he replies, and my heart seizes a little at the sound of that.

But still, I follow my instincts. Shut the car door behind me and leave him there while I walk inside, alone. Because I know I'm doing the right thing, hard as it may be when my lips and my body are both singing at the memory of him.

The last thing in the world I need is to start developing feelings for Jasper Quint.

****

"I don't understand, you're going to need to say this slower."

93

On the other end of the phone, I can hear Melissa chewing the spoonful of cereal she's eating as we both watch our favorite wind-down trashy reality shows. Her after a long day of nannying, and me after a long day of, well…

"Basically the owner's obsessed with family."

"Antoine Quint," she replies. "I don't live under a rock, Dee. But you're saying he's forcing his son to… what, just jump on the first wife opportunity that comes along?"

"When I say obsessed, I mean really, truly he doesn't think his son can run a business without a wife." I twirl my spoon between my fingertips, the ice cream I'm eating poised forgotten on my thigh. "Which, actually, after spending the whole day touring the place with Jasper, I can't say I don't

94

understand…"

"Jasper. You're on a first-name basis with Jasper Quint. You've been hired to pretend to *marry* Jasper Quint."

"I know it sounds crazy—"

"It *is* crazy, Dee. You know I love you, and I'll support you no matter what, but have you considered how this will look on your résumé once you leave? 'Yes, Ms. Smith, how did your first internship go?' 'Well, I married and then divorced the head of the company…'"

"It's not going to be a *real* wedding. We'll just play-act until his dad hands over the CEO-ship, and then go our separate ways. Plus he's going to write me a letter of recommendation specially—"

"Recommending you for what, wife of the

year?" But I can hear the amusement in her voice. Not to mention the tap of keyboard keys.

"What are you doing?" I ask, suddenly suspicious.

"Googling your hubby-to-be, of course, as any good friend would do."

I groan. "Melissa…"

"Holy shit girl." I hear the click-click-click of her keyboard as she scrolls through images. "Okay, I revise my earlier stance. Husband that immediately. Is he really that good-looking in person?"

I snort. "I mean… He's not *not*. But he's also a, a…" I think back to our tour today. The way he leaned in in the car, adrenaline racing through our veins, and for a moment, I could imagine the taste of his lips, the feel of that scratchy five o'clock shadow against my cheek... "I don't know. He's too flirty. Too forward."

She laughs, too. "I'm sorry, are these *bad* things?"

"It's a business transaction! He's blurring the lines. That's a red flag."

"Mhmmm." Melissa's tone on the far end sounds far too knowing for my taste. "Well, I hope you enjoy your *business transaction*. You've got to keep me posted on how much you enjoy blurring the lines once your new hubby gets you into the wedding night bed—"

"I've got to go now," I call into the phone, though we're both cracking up.

"Also, you need to tell me if his hair still looks that good after he's been rolling around in the sack all night—"

"Goodbye, Melissa."

"Love you, Dee."

"Love you too." I hang up with a groan and an eye roll. But I can't deny it. I'm smiling, too, ear-to-ear. And that makes me more nervous than anything else.

CHAPTER FOUR

Jasper

I tell my father I'm going out of town for the weekend. Then I leave several brochures for the romantic getaway I've planned for me and Dee, all in very obvious places, so that Dad will be sure to stumble across them. Nosy as he is about my personal life, he won't be able to resist asking around, and Greg will be all too happy to report that I'm out of town with a girl I've been courting. A girl, who Greg will tell my father, I'm actually serious about for once.

We figure this will help cement the lie that we eloped, once we finally spring our marriage on my father in time for the family reunion. Which is in three weeks' time now—not a moment to lose.

I sent Dee a text inviting her to meet me at the office and bring a suitcase for the weekend. I figure that if Dad doesn't get nosy and snoop around, at least this will stir up enough office gossip to reach his ear before I return on Sunday evening, hopefully engaged. Well, fake engaged, but still.

Now to just put the finishing touches on the weekend. I call ahead to the resort and request the honeymoon suite. There's a little back-and-forth, until I drop the surname Quint, and then suddenly, "Oh of course, Mr. Quint, not a problem at all, of course it's free."

I have to hide a smile when I disconnect. Normally I hate to pull that card, but it does come in handy, at times.

Especially in situations like this. Situations where I'm about to go away for the weekend with a woman I cannot get out of my head.

The moment I first saw her, sitting in Greg's office in an outfit that looked like she found it on a sale rack at Target, sounding desperate while she talked about her college plans, I knew she'd be perfect. Just the unwitting gold-digger type my family would hate. Lack of class and poor and all.

But the more I got to know her, giving her the office tour and listening to her ramble about the cars like she'd grown up under the hood of one, the more I started to realize... I could actually like this woman.

The way she handled the stick shift on the test track, I have to admit, made my own stick shift hard as a rock to watch. I've never seen anyone drive like that—well, anyone except yours truly. And the kiss we shared afterward, her pert little mouth hot against mine, her tongue curling my own. She wanted it. She wanted it as bad as I did, I could feel it, taste it in that kiss.

And then she pulled back, walked away, and it's been all I can do not to text her constantly or linger around the offices where the other interns are working to try and catch glimpses of her. I spotted her near the water cooler the other day, in a perfectly work appropriate top that still made me think all kinds of naughty thoughts.

I keep coming up with excuses to text her— first I had to compliment her on a small job the intern supervisor tells me was very well done. Then I had to ask for her preference on getaway locations ("outdoorsy but not too I'm-going-to-murder-you-in-the-middle-of-nowhere," she'd replied, which led me to pick this amazing little seaside resort town over a cabin in the woods type). Then I had to find out her dress size, since obviously she won't be packing anything we'll be able to wear to a decent restaurant in town.

Then I had to ask about her favorite movies, and what she thought about the cars, and if she's changed her mind at all on the whole business aspect of our business arrangement. The last one, I'll admit, I asked during a moment of weakness late on night, after far too many replays danced through my head of her legs under that tight dress she wore to her first day, and the faint little sigh she let out when our lips parted from our kiss.

I couldn't help imagining everything else I wanted to do to her in that car. How I wanted to drag her into the backseat and peel that dress off, and cover her with something far more appealing—my mouth. I'd lick and suck my way down to her breasts, cup them one after the other, all while I parted her thighs with my hand and made sure she was wet and ready to drive my thick cock next...

I'm getting hard against just thinking about it, and I have to shut my eyes and lean back in my desk chair and take a few deep, steadying breaths.

That's when there's a knock at my door, of course. My eyes snap open, and I find Dee there in the doorway, head tilted in confusion as she watches me.

"Um, you asked me to meet you here..." she says.

"In half an hour." I dart a glance at the clock. No, I'm not mistaken. She's just early.

Her cheeks flush. "Greg suggested I come early, in case..." She trails off, then, and glances out the open door, back toward the hallway. "Um, should I?"

I nod, and she steps inside, and the air in my office seems to warm by at least fifteen degrees. She's wearing a much cuter dress today than her interview outfit, a clingy little sundress that reveals the enticing slope of her neck, the curve of her bare shoulders, and more than enough hints to guess at the perfect, perky size of her breasts beneath all that cleavage.

She perches on the edge of the chair on the

other side of my desk, like she's nervous to relax her muscles, let her guard down at all. I know the feeling. She makes me feel the same way.

"Uh, Greg suggested if I came by sooner, more people might see us talking, or waiting for the car out front. You know, to maximize, um, visibility."

"I see." I stand and step around to the closer side of the desk. From here, I catch the delicate scent of her perfume, mingled with the sweeter, headier scent underneath, the one that's all *her*. "Good suggestion. So why are we closed in my office?" I arch a brow, a smirk dancing at the edges of my lips.

I don't miss the way her breath catches, or the way her gaze dips to my chest, down past my abs, to the V of my groin. Then her eyes jump back to my face, her cheeks redder than ever. God, she's sexy

when she's blushing. "Right. Yeah. Sorry. Of course."
She shoves to her feet. "I just thought we should…"

I reach up to catch the same stray strand of
hair that escaped her messy bun last time, and tuck it
behind her ear, making sure to let my fingertip graze
her earlobe, ever so slightly. I notice the way she
shivers, mouth parted in an almost inaudible sigh.
"You thought we should catch up in private first?" I
ask, eyes alight with mischief. "Maybe take up where
we left off last time, and make sure our chemistry is
believable?"

"Let's save the chemistry for when we have an
audience," she replies, and with that, she sidesteps me,
and reaches for the door handle.

Together we step back out into the lobby, and
the moment we do, I catch her hand. She tenses for a

moment, like she's startled, and then relaxes into it, even curls her fingers through mine for an added touch.

Even just this faint touch of her soft skin is enough to drive me wild. Because I can imagine holding this hand above her head. Pinning her in place with one hand while I cup my other around her cheek, pull her in for a long, deep kiss; the kind of kiss that leads to my hand sliding under that dress of hers, and her undoing the button of my jeans…

I need to stop this train of thought before I make it difficult to walk around the office.

"So, I packed the things you suggested," she says, her voice forcefully light. "Bathing suit, a nice dress. Any hints about where we're going yet?"

I smirk. "Don't worry, it's not in the middle

of nowhere."

She half-smiles. "Okay, so one point in the not-murdery sounding direction. Any other details you'd care to share?"

"It's one of my favorite places in the world."

"Really? Why's that, do you enjoy sneaking off there with all of your fake wives?"

She asks the last question a little too loudly, and I elbow her, even though so far it's just us striding across the lobby and Caroline, our receptionist, in the distance eying our clasped hands with what I figure is more interest than usual. Good. If anyone's going to immediately tell the rest of the office about what she just saw, it's Caroline. She's a little bit over-the-top, and a little bit still pissed at me for the drunken one-night stand we had years ago, but hey, sometimes that gossipy mouth of hers can work in your favor.

I turn away, back to Dee and her question. "Because I used to go there as a kid," I say, surprising myself. "With my parents, back before Dad took over the company and started his now crazy work schedule."

Her eyebrows rise. "You and your father are close?"

"Of course." I frown at her sideways.

She lowers her eyes, a little embarrassed. "I just sort of assumed that, I mean, given the nature of this whole thing..." She squeezes my hand. "That you were being like, forced into something you didn't want."

"I'd say coerced more than forced," I reply. "And you can care about family without agreeing to their every demand, no?"

She laughs a little at that. "I suppose." Her expression turns wistful, and I remember what she told me last time about driving cars in the countryside with her father.

"What about you?" I ask. "Are you close to your family?"

"I was." Her expression darkens, like a cloud, and I regret asking. The last thing I want to do is cause her pain. "My parents both passed away."

"I'm so sorry to hear that." I stop walking.

So does she. She stares at her feet instead, and breathes in deep. "I just…" She blinks a couple of times and then forces a big smile. "Sometimes I just miss having them around, you know? But I'm doing well now. Just… You know, something like that, it makes you realize how important every day is. Live life to the fullest, and all that." She flashes me a grin. "And never take for granted the time you do have with your family, even if they annoy the hell out of you."

"Amen to that." I tug her closer to me, and we start to walk again, our arms brushing. I can't stop thinking about her smile, though. How bravely she goes through the world after something as devastating as her parents' loss must have been.

I realize I'm watching her from the corner of my eye, checking to see if she's okay, but she's doing better than I am, staring through the front windows with widening eyes.

"Oh my God," she says, interrupting my reverie on the importance of love and the pain of loss. "Is that a first-generation Andromeda?" Her voice shoots up an octave.

I laugh. "My father's car," I say. "I asked to borrow it for this trip."

"We get to *ride in it?*"

No need to worry about how we're going to attract enough attention to get noticed. Every eye in the building swivels in our direction now as her voice echoes in the lobby. And then she's dropping my hand and peeling straight for the sliding glass doors to ogle the car. Which, I have to admit, with its cherry red paint and sleek design, is more than enough to distract anyone who's into this sort of thing.

Watching her geek out, though, is doing funny things to my head. Funny things like making me imagine what she'd do if I caught her mid-step and swung her onto the hood of this car, then wrapped those lithe, strong legs of hers around my waist and pulled her tight, curvy body against mine.

Dee circles the car, and I follow her, trying not to focus too hard on the way her ass moves in that slim-fitting dress. Or how much better she'd look without that dress on at all…

"Is this original?" she calls, pointing out some of the features the Andromeda is known for.

I nod, and grin at her wide-eyed gasp of appreciation. "You know, not many people would get this excited over a car."

"Not many people have ever gotten to ride in a car like this one," she counters, and with that, she reaches down to lift her suitcase into the backseat, since the convertible top is already down.

"Oh no." I step around the car and grab the bag from her before she gets it higher than waist-height. "That's not your job."

"Going to do all my heavy lifting for me this trip too?" Her eyebrows rise. "What a gentleman."

"Me? No." I snap my fingers. In an instant, one of the valets we have on stand-by at this lot appears at my side. "This is practice," I tell her, as I pass the suitcase off to him to pack into the car. "Where we're going, my family has a reputation, and there are things you don't handle yourself. Thank you, Pierre," I add in an aside to the valet, while slipping him a $20 tip clutched between two fingers.

"Valet service in your own parking lot?" She lifts an eyebrow at me. "That seems a bit extra, Quint."

"This is Quint Motors. We specialize in extra."

With that, I open the passenger side door for Dee. "You're going to have to figure out how to behave around my family if we want to pull this off," I explain. Or rather, I don't expect her to pick this up, and I expect it to cause friction all over the place as soon as we touch down in Greece for the family reunion. But I'm not about to let her in on that little plan—the plan for my entire family to hate the idea of her so much that they'll be relieved when I "divorce" her, and apologetic for forcing me into such a rushed marriage in the first place.

With one last glance at the lobby—packed with people now, because Friday lunch hour has just begun, and everyone's eager to race to the parking lot and away from here to whatever lunch plans they've made—I'm satisfied we've put in enough of an appearance for the day. I slide into the driver's seat and steer us onto the highway up the coast, toward the tiny town of Newholme.

****

We pull into Newholme from the highway far above town just as the sun is setting out over the water. Dee gasps at the sight of it, and even I have to admit, this is a better sunset than usual in a town known for its sunsets. It's like she's my lucky charm.

The town itself looks picturesque, a bunch of candy-colored beach houses lining white sand beaches and the deep blue waves of the Pacific beyond.

"It's so beautiful," she sighs as we turn toward

town, down a long road that leads to the little—okay, not so little—hotel where we'll be staying for the weekend. Soon enough, we're turning up the winding drive into the main complex, and her eyes widen, if possible, still further. "Jasper, you know we're not on our fake honeymoon yet, right?"

"Ah, about that." I bite the inside of my cheek to suppress a smile.

Somehow, she sees right through me anyway. She narrows her eyes at me in the rearview mirror. "Tell me you didn't book the honeymoon suite."

"It's good practice. Besides, the honeymoon suite is two rooms, so I can stay on the couch, assuming you're still opposed to this business relationship becoming any more interesting business."

She narrows her eyes still further. "I told you,

I signed on to be your fake wife. Not a real one—and not some hookup either."

I shrug one shoulder and toss her a grin. "Can't blame a guy for trying."

She rolls her eyes. "Keep dreaming, Mr. Quint."

"Oh, I do, future Mrs. Quint." I flash her a wink, and she groans aloud. But when I look her way again, I notice a smile playing around the corners of her lips, before she wipes it away with a serious expression.

"Okay, so what's the game plan?"

I can't help it. I burst into laughter. "The game plan is, we go down into the town tomorrow and find you a proper engagement ring. Something gaudy enough to be believable. Then we… Well." I gesture broadly toward the scenery below us. "Amuse ourselves for a couple of days, and return to the offices amidst a swirl of rumors. Hopefully. Greg has promised to speed a few of those whispers up, naturally."

"Naturally." She laughs. "What is he, your assistant or your pimp?"

"Little bit of everything, like any good assistant." I smirk at her, and she peels off into laughter again.

God, I love that sound.

And fuck, I really shouldn't.

We pull into the hotel drive, and this time, I'm pleased to note that Dee waits for the chauffeur to open her door before she tries bounding out all on her own. Not to mention, she doesn't even reach for

the trunk or her own bag. She's learning quickly.
Good.

Or, possibly not good, if she adapts a little
too fast. Maybe I should stop offering her lessons on
how to woo the high and mighty rich, and instead try
to bring out her down-home country side as often as
possible around my family.

But I find myself unable to help it. Even
though I know she needs to not get along with my
family, and our time at the reunion needs to be a
disaster, part of me wants her to enjoy herself there.
To have a good time. To impress my parents.

As the bellhop whisks our suitcases upstairs,
she turns to me, then, suddenly suspicious says, "You
said tomorrow we'd go to the jewelers."

I nod. "This is a small town. Most of the

shops have already closed for the day."

"But, what are we going to do for the rest of tonight, then?"

I grin. "That's where my aforementioned assistant's planning skills come in handy." I offer her a hand. She slides her fingers through mine, with only one hesitant glance at the distant clerk manning the hotel entrance. "Right this way."

I lead her down the cobblestone road that winds down beside the hotel, leaving the car in the capable hands of the valet. He's a friend of the family, and I know he's far too familiar with my father to damage the car my dad's known for.

The cobblestone road is foot traffic only, mostly empty at this hour, save for a couple of other lovebirds strolling along, arms linked and heads bent close to one another in conversation. In the distance, out over the water, we watch the sun sink toward the horizon, until finally the waves swallow it whole, and the sky is painted bright neon pinks and yellows and oranges in its wake.

"Sunset was my mother's favorite time of day," Dee volunteers, after we've walked a few more paces, nearly to the stairs down the side of the hill on which the hotel is perched. Halfway down is the turn-off we need. "She used to make me turn off the TV and come join her on the porch for every one. Every single night. Of course, our view wasn't much compared to this one." Dee laughs and gestures toward the ocean.

I shrug, arm brushing against hers. "Still the same sun, and the same waves to set over."

She flashes me a surprised smile. "That's what my mom always used to say. Well. Not exactly, but whenever I'd complain about not having the latest phone, or not having dresses as nice as the other girls at school… She'd say we all wake up under the same sky and fall asleep looking at the same moon."

"Smart woman." I smile.

"She was." Dee's eyes soften, as she holds my gaze.

I step closer, and for a second, I think maybe she's going to crack. Let me through that hard exterior that I know she's projecting because she wants to keep things between us strictly professional. Even if she's tempted to do otherwise.

But then Dee turns away and steps back down the path, tugging me along after her.

"Right here," I say, and she leads the way, drawing me down a side path off the main road until we reach my favorite restaurant. Nestled halfway down the hill into town, with a back porch that juts out over the hill, it looks like someone's grandmother's cottage. If not for the uniformed staff member standing beside the door, you'd mistake it for a private residence.

"What is this place?" she murmurs, as we step inside and the hostess waves us through.

"Restaurant owned by the same chef who runs Sicile, back in the city."

Her eyes widen. "Isn't he famous?" she whispers, just low enough for me to hear, as we trail after the hostess and out onto the back porch.

"Very," I confirm, and then smile as we step

up to the little two-top I reserved for us, with a view of the bay below, the lingering pink clouds from sunset, and the lights winking on all across town in cottage and villa windows. Poised here, we could already be on the edge of the Mediterranean Sea, it looks so much like Greece. "My father is close friends with him. Their great-grandfathers grew up together."

She flashes me a smile. "Everything seems to be about family connections with you."

"Everything is," I respond, and close my menu without a glance. "We'll both do the chef's choice," I tell the waitress, who appeared a split second after the hostess.

Under the table, Dee kicks me. "How do you know I don't have any allergies?"

I hold up a hand to stall the waitress. "My

apologies. Do you have any allergies?"

She flattens her lips for a moment. "No. But I might have."

I laugh and then smile at the waitress, who flashes me a wink when she thinks Dee isn't looking and disappears to go place our orders.

"Does everybody do that around you?" Dee asks. "Or just pretty women?"

"Do what?" I ask with a grin.

"Give you whatever you want."

"Hmm. Some pretty women do." I study her for a long moment, making sure to let my gaze drop to the neckline of her gown. "Others are more withholding. Less open to adventure and exploration."

She groans. "I just don't want things to get

complicated."

"We're faking an elopement. Things are already complicated."

"Well, any *more* complicated, then."

"Some things are worth complicating." I wink.

"I hate when you do that," she complains.

"You don't like winking?"

"No, I don't like when you… make me…" She groans. "Why am I second-guessing myself? Why are you so damned… *you*?" She waves a hand in my general direction.

"If it makes you feel any better, you aren't the only distracted one."

Her cheeks flare, if possible, redder than ever before. "Great. So we both have bad judgment."

"I wouldn't say that. Unless there's something

about you I don't know." I tilt my head to one side, grinning. "Some horrible secret that would make you unmarriageable."

"You mean besides the fact that I agreed to marry a guy for money and a letter of recommendation for college?" She bursts into laughter, which only gets worse when the waitress appears at our table, eyes huge enough to indicate that she must have overheard at least part of our conversation.

"A private joke," I explain as I slide my hand across the table to take Dee's once more.

She lets me, and continues to hold on after the waitress departs. I trace my thumb over the back of her hand in slow circles, marveling at how soft and smooth her skin is. How perfect and unmarred.

"I've never been in love," she says, unbidden.

My eyebrows shoot upward. "Are you faking the break-up already, because that doesn't come until after the faux honeymoon, you know."

"No, I mean…" She flushes. Damn. It's distracting as fuck when she blushes like that. Especially when she tilts her head to one side and chews on her lip, as she's doing now, eyes downcast, like she doesn't even realize what she's doing to me. It takes every ounce of my self-control not to tighten my grip on her hand. Drag her across this table and into my lap. "You asked what makes me unmarriageable. I've never been in love before. I don't even know if I'm capable of it. I mean, I like sex, don't get me wrong—"

"Thank God for that," I interrupt, though I

have to admit, hearing her say the word *sex* makes my already tight pants uncomfortably tighter. I've imagined that too much, too many times already, for it not to go straight to my head—my southern head.

She laughs, and flashes me a look that's half-glare, half something else. Something underneath that feigned annoyance that looks a whole lot like the same desire curling through my body. "But I've never felt more. All that romantic stuff you're supposed to feel. The stuff my parents felt."

I know that feeling. "Sounds to me like you just haven't met the right person yet." I lift one shoulder, let it drop.

She scrunches up her forehead. "Or the right person for me doesn't exist."

"Now, now." I lean forward and catch her

under the chin with two fingers. Tilt her head back until her eyes snap to mine. "There is definitely somebody for you, my dear. Face like yours?" I search it. Commit it to memory. Her eyes, too, the way they widen now and catch the light, little perfect pools of blue that someone you could lose yourself in far too easily. *She's dangerous.* It makes me want her more. "I'm surprised there isn't already a line out the door, waiting for you to take your pick of suitors."

For a breath, she doesn't move, eyes locked on mine. Her lips parts, just a hair, and I start to lean toward her.

Then the waitress reappears with our food, and she snaps back to the present, leans away from me, head bent so her hair tumbles forward out of its hold and disguises her face. "I'm not the kind of girl guys chase," she murmurs to her plate. "I'm more of the best friend type. The one who encourages them to chase the girl they really want."

"Hmm." I lean back in my chair and study her, not even bothering to pick up my fork yet. I'm not interested in the food anymore, even though this is one of my favorite restaurants around. Right now, she's all I see. "If you ask me, those guys are blind, then."

She laughs, and her face lights up with it, and I realize… I'm in trouble here.

CHAPTER FIVE

Dee

I force Jasper to sleep on the couch.

Well, *force* is a strong word. More like, we get back from dinner, my head dizzy from his stares, his compliments, and the food, which tasted better than anything I think I've ever put in my mouth before. *Anything except Jasper's tongue,* my unhelpful subconscious points out.

And then I made a beeline straight for the bedroom and shut the door between us. Just in case he got any ideas about bidding me goodnight, I locked it for good measure.

It's the honeymoon suite, far too enormous for its own good, so there's a full en suite bathroom out in the living room anyway. And even though I locked my pitiable overnight back out there with Jasper, there's more than enough supplies scattered throughout the honeymoon suite to tide me over for the night. I brush my teeth with the hotel's toothbrush, wash my face with their soap—which is nicer than the dollar store stuff I packed, and put on one of the hotel's cozy nightgowns. The one with the Mrs. stitched over the lapel. For a moment, I smile at it in the mirror, thinking of the joke Jasper would make.

Then I chide myself. Why am I still thinking about him?

Why have I *been* thinking about him, nonstop,

every day at the office hoping and praying to catch a glimpse of him, then lighting up every time he texts me. All week he's been stuck in my damn head, ever since that disastrous kiss after we went racing around the test track last week.

Disastrous... and impossible to forget.

He kisses like he's dying of thirst, and I'm an oasis. He kisses like he'd like to drown in me, and I've never been kissed like that before, not by anybody.

I meant what I told him at dinner—I've never fallen in love. I don't even know if I can. But the last thing I want to do right now is to develop real feelings for the guy I'm pretending to be married to for work. So even though I spent the last week dreaming about what I'd do alone in a hotel room with Jasper—or rather, dreaming about what he could do to me, with those big, strong hands of his, and that chiseled, perfectly sculpted body... Not to mention the sizable cock I've glimpsed through his jeans when I surprised him in his office and realized he must have been doing some daydreaming of his own.

God, think about how that thing would feel between my thighs right now, with me spread-eagled across the bed, him poised over me, those hooded, dark eyes studying me, drinking me in, like he did all throughout dinner...

I shove that thought to the back of my mind and stay in my bedroom alone instead.

I do, however, slide a hand down my panties while I think about him out there on the couch. I imagine joining him. Throwing caution to the wind and complicating the fuck out of this situation. I think about his lips on mine, his hand where mine is now, spreading the lips of my wet pussy and pressing between the folds, delving into me again and again, his finger thicker than mine, moving faster, harder, enough to make me cry out in delight—

Shit. I freeze, heart pounding, chest heaving, fingers still inside my wet, hot, clenched pussy. Because I just did just that. Screamed out loud.

I hold still, hold my breath, and listen through the pounding in my ears for any sound from the other room. *Did he hear that?* Does he know what I'm doing in here and why?

Finally, after far too many minutes of waiting, I decide he must already be asleep. Thank God.

Only then do I push off the bed and head for

the shower. I turn the handle all the way to cold, and only warm it up once the icy water has washed up away any remaining fantasies and desires. But at last, when I do turn in, sleep eludes me. I stare at the ceiling, and my mind just keeps drifting back to the same spot. Back to the temptation I know I need to resist...

****

Over breakfast, Jasper keeps shooting me sly smiles. "You look lovely this morning," he says, in a way that instantly makes me suspicious.

"Don't know why; I barely slept," I mumble through a mouthful of scalding hot tea. I wince and set the cup back down to give it more time to cool off.

"No?" He lifts a brow. "I always found the beds here comfortable. That is, unless you were... distracted."

My face feels hot. "What on earth would I have to be distracted about?"

He shrugs one shoulder, casual. "Maybe you were in there regretting locking me out. Missing all the sleep we could have been avoiding together."

This time, I gulp too much tea to disguise my reaction, even though I'm sure my face gives me away. Jasper laughs. *Bastard.* But he's right, of course. "Oh, so you *weren't* fantasizing about me out there on the couch all alone?" I lift a brow.

His smirk only widens. "So you admit *you* were thinking about *me.*"

I roll my eyes. Damn him. "That's not what I meant."

"Well, if it's any consolation, I was definitely thinking about you." His hand brushes my knee under the table, lightly, and I jump at the sudden shock of his touch. "Thinking about my sexy little wife, and that blush she gets on her face, and the way she chews her lower lip—yes, just like that." He winks.

I stop biting my lip and glare instead.

"Mm. I wonder which face is closer to the expression you'd make if I were making you come?"

Now my jaw drops open entirely. "Jasper—"

"I mean, I already know what you sound like when you orgasm, after last night."

I close my eyes and snap my mouth closed again too. *Dammit.* "I was just... it... that..."

"Don't feel embarrassed, Dee. I was doing the same thing, you know." He catches my eye, his own dark and serious. "Thinking about you last night at dinner. Thinking about peeling that dress off your tight little body, and watching you ride my big cock while I fucked you on the couch. That's what I was thinking. What about you?"

His words go straight to my pussy. My belly tightens, and I can already feel myself growing damp between the legs. I struggle to contain my breathing, to keep my heart from racing. The waiter walks by, and I seize on that distraction, flag him down for a refill of tea, which buys me enough time to somewhat recover.

"Can we have some breakfast menus?" I ask the waiter, all the while fixing Jasper with a pointed stare. "That's what I've been unable to stop thinking about all night. Breakfast."

"Um… Sure thing, miss," the waiter says, only after a confused glance between us.

Jasper's still smirking at me, damn him. But he doesn't say anything, only turns his attention to the menu, and behaves himself for the rest of our morning meal. At least until we leave for the car. Then he rests his hand on the small of my back, his skin warm against mine. I jump a little, then relax into the touch, smiling at the hotel attendees we pass, as I remember the charade we're supposed to be maintaining right now.

"No need to look so concerned," he murmurs beside my ear. "Your obvious attraction to me does us favors in this case."

I sigh in response, though I can't resist biting my lip and shooting him a long sideways glance. "You're more attractive when you don't admit to knowing it so much," I point out in response, which earns me a chuckle from him.

He steers me out to the car, which is just as impressive as it was the first time I laid eyes on it. Part of me still can't believe this is my life—riding around in luxury vehicles with the son of the magnate who makes them. *And getting paid to pretend to be his wife*, part of my brain points out. An unhelpful part.

In town, we stroll hand-in-hand through the winding little streets. It's adorable here, like something straight out of a movie set. I fall in love with the charming little seaside cafés and shops interspersed between them. Part of me wants to beg Jasper to stop in one of those stores to browse the cutesy little ocean-themed souvenirs—I'm a sucker for seashells. But I resist the urge. Today we're on a mission.

"So. Engagement rings." Jasper cuts me a sideways glance. "What's your style? Vintage, modern, something gaudy or flashy?"

"I... I don't know. I've never really given it much consideration."

"Ah, yes, I forgot, the whole never been in love thing. Never daydreamed about your wedding either?"

I shake my head. "Not really the type."

"At least that will make our elopement story more believable." He winks and leads me by the hand into a jewelry store that looks fancier than any place I've ever bothered to set foot inside. I know I'd never be able to afford even the smallest piece of jewelry in a place like this, so why bother?

Still, I can't help but admit, it is beautiful. We cross the broad, sunlit lobby, a skylight shining down above us, and an attendee crosses the floor to assist us. "What can I do for you today?" he asks with a broad smile.

"We're shopping for a ring for the lovely lady here," Jasper answers, leaning down to kiss my temple. I notice he lingers there a second, lips against my skin, and I can't help closing my eyes in pleasure. "We're getting married next weekend, so it needs to be one on short-order."

"Of course, of course." The attendee's face positively lights up. "Right this way, and I'll show you the selection we have in stock. Do you know your

ring size, Ms. ...?" He waits, expectant, and I realize
he's waiting for my name.

"Oh, Dee. Hi."

"Ms. Dee." He smiles. "And the lucky
husband-to-be?"

"Jasper," he replies. "Jasper Quint."

Neither of us can miss the startled, then even
more pleased look that chases its way across the
jeweler's face. I can already imagine the dollar signs
that must be popping up in his imagination. "Well,
Mr. Quint, Ms. Dee—"

"Just Dee, thanks," I interrupt. "And no, I
don't know my ring size."

"Let's just get you sized right over here then."
He leads us into a side room, sumptuously decorated.
With a single gesture, he magically summons several

other attendants, one bearing a tray of cookies, another with pots of tea and coffee. I accept a cookie, then watch Jasper wave them off, saying "No thank you, we just ate."

Embarrassed, I try to replace the cookie on the tray, but he catches me and rolls his eyes. "Don't stand on ceremony with me, darling. If you want the cookie, eat the cookie."

I shrug and take a larger-than-is-strictly-ladylike bite in response. Then my eyes flutter closed in pleasure. *Oh God.* Even the cookies in this place are amazing. What do they do, partner with a bakery?

"My wife makes those," the attendant explains, with a grin in my direction. "Best chocolate cookies in Newholme, if you ask me."

"Oh, they are." I finish it off in one more

bite, and Jasper laughs.

"Sweet tooth, huh? Good to know."

"What are you, taking notes?" I shoot back at him.

"Maybe." Jasper grins at me. "It's best to know all of your preferences. Speaking of which." He eyes the table, and I realize the other attendants have laid out a veritable spread of rings.

They look almost as delicious as the chocolate cookies—albeit a hell of a lot more expensive. I gape at them, because each seems more beautiful than the last, each rock bigger, each setting more ornate.

"They're all so pretty…" I begin, hesitant.

"To your right here, we have the princess cut diamonds," the jeweler begins to explain. "A more traditional look, some of these have vintage settings

149

too—this ruby here, for example, with the diamonds around it, was actually from an older eighteenth century ring, which we reset after the original band was damaged. But most of our rings are newly made, such as…"

I zone out, because halfway through scanning the table, one ring in particular has caught my eye. It's smaller than some of the others, not as showy maybe, but to me, it's beautiful. The center stone is a diamond, oval-cut, but around it are dozens of tiny sapphires in little wings, so they make the central stone look like the center of a beautiful, intricate flower. Without thinking, I reach for it, lips parted a little as I hold it up to the light.

"You like that one?" Jasper asks, his eyes bright and flashing in the store light.

I look from the ring to him and back again. Like him, this ring is a little dark. A little complicated. A lot attractive. I swallow hard, and set it back on the table. "Yes. But, I don't know, I don't know anything about diamonds, really…"

"That is a lovely ring," the jeweler agrees with a smile. "But perhaps you might prefer this one here. If you like the oval cuts, this stone has brighter clarity, and it's a few more carats." He flashes a significant look at Jasper then, and we all understand the subtext. *This is more expensive.*

He shows me another oval ring—also beautiful, of course, as they all are. He holds this one out to me, and I offer my finger. It slides right on, a perfect fit.

"Do you like that one, or would you prefer

151

the other?" Jasper asks me, as though this is a serious question. As though it matters for anything other than the show we're putting on.

"Whatever you like," I reply. "They're both nice." But my gaze drifts back to the sapphire ring anyway, in spite of myself.

"We'll take the second one then," Jasper says, and my heart sinks a little in disappointment.

Though again, I don't know why. It's just a ring. Just a fake engagement ring, which I'll be returning at the end of a couple weeks when this ridiculous charade is over. *It doesn't matter*. So I plaster a broad smile onto my face and pretend to be pleased, as we settle up the bill, and Jasper pockets the ring.

"Shouldn't I wear it?" I ask, eyebrow lifted. "I thought that was the whole reason for buying it."

"You should wear it," he agrees. "Though not until I properly give it to you." His eyes sparkle, then, and I have a feeling he's got mischief on his mind.

****

We wind up at a little bar on the boardwalk, way out on the tip of the pier that juts out over the sea. Ocean breezes drift past us, and overhead, the sun is dipping toward the horizon, already painting the clouds orange with its passing. We're still waiting on our drink order—a bottle of champagne, chilled on ice, and a brand that I've never actually been able to drink, only ogle on magazine covers, due to the steep price tag—when Jasper suddenly swings around on his feet to face me.

"Dee."

"Oh God," I say in response.

He drops to one knee. "I know we've only known one another for a short time now."

My face immediately goes hot. I hear whispers start up around us, a few squeals of delight. Total strangers whip out cameras and flashes start going off all around. "I can't believe you're actually doing this," I hiss under my breath, though I can't help the faint smile that touches my lips.

It *is* kind of funny.

And embarrassing. Mostly embarrassing.

But funny.

"In the short time we've been acquainted, you have swept me off my feet," Jasper says, eyes locked on mine. "I've fallen for you, head over heels. For your love of cars, and your death-wish when you drive those cars."

I snort and roll my eyes. But when he holds up a hand, I extend my left one, and let him grip it tight.

"I've fallen for your sense of humor, and the way you're glaring at me all the time," he continues.

Now I'm outright laughing. To my surprise, I can't drag my gaze from his, either. I'm stuck here, watching him propose and wondering… *How much of what I'm feeling is real?*

"I love you, Dee Smith," he says, and he draws the ring from his pocket, the diamond flashing in the setting sun. It throws stars in my eyes. Blinds me, until all I can see is Jasper. "Will you marry me?"

I pause. Take a moment to survey our

onlookers, who cheer and whistle. More cameras flash in my eyes. Then I look back to Jasper, and take a deep breath. *Here goes nothing.* "Well, Jasper Quint," I say, loud enough that neighboring tables will be able to overhear. If we're going to sell this performance in public, we may as well put it to good use. Maybe some of those gossip rags will get wind of the heir to Quint Motors' engagement and spread word to his father. "You don't leave me much choice, I have to admit." I flash him a wink. "But given all your insistence, I have to say… yes. I'll marry you."

He slides the ring on my finger, and pulls me to my feet all in one motion. Before I can protest, he cups my chin in one hand and tilts it up to his. Then his lips are on mine again, and I don't *want* to protest. I want to sink into this moment, stay here forever. I want this kiss to keep going. I want his warm hands to circle my waist, slide down, farther.

I want to be alone with him, back in our hotel room, where I can tear that stupid tie off him and rip the buttons off his probably too-expensive shirt, and run my hands over his hot, bare skin, the way I've been itching to do ever since our last kiss.

I wrap both arms around his neck, pull him to me, as he deepens the kiss, and I nip his lower lip, a hint at what I want, a hint at *more*.

Then the waiter reappears with the champagne, and a cork pops, and the cheers explode into full-blown applause, with mixed whispers of *Jasper Quint* thrown in and circulating the growing crowd, and finally, we pull apart, both of us breathless, eyes glazed, a little stunned, as we drop back into our seats, and allow the congratulations to wash over us.

CHAPTER SIX

Dee

We stop back at the hotel to change before dinner. Unlike last night, we're going somewhere showy, celebratory. Jasper brought me a dress, he informs me once we reach the suite, and he hands it to me without looking, without an offer to trail me into the bedroom this time. His usual flirtation and overly sexy commentary faded this afternoon—ever since his proposal and the kiss that followed. Both of us are a little quieter after that. Shell-shocked.

I can't stop thinking about the way he made my heart beat faster, the way he tasted, and the way...

The way I felt like I had butterflies in my stomach. I've never felt like that before. I've never had feelings like that for anybody, even guys I'm attracted to. *What on earth is wrong with me?*

Then again, nobody has ever proposed to me before. Maybe I've just never been forced into a ridiculously romantic situation like that before. Maybe I'd feel like this about anybody who got down on one knee and slipped an enormous diamond onto my finger.

Still, I can't help wishing that Jasper's prior flirtation would return. After that kiss, I might actually be tempted to let him get away with something right now.

But he stands by the door of the living room like a perfect gentleman, picking out a new "evening tie" while I slip past into the bedroom.

The moment I unwrap the gown, I have to laugh. It's just so *not me*. I wear dresses, don't get me wrong, but not like this. Floor-length, satin, with a sweeping neckline and crystals studded along the hemline. It would almost look like a wedding gown if it weren't a deep mauve. A beautiful color, but not me.

Still. Duty calls. This is what I signed up for, after all. Pass as a rich girl in a rich world. So I step into the gown and draw it up—it fits me perfectly. I have to admit, Jasper is good at sizing people up. I gave him my dress size, but this is a really close fit, a risky buy. Unless he's been studying my curves…

160

Stop thinking about that, I scold myself. I fix the ring on my finger—it does go with the dress, I note, though it's the only thing about me that does. Then I do up my hair, and finally I reach over my shoulder...

And find I can't reach the zipper on the gown. It's too low, nestled at the small of my back.

I glance at the door. Take a deep breath, and cross over to it. "Jasper?" I call softly through the crack.

"Ready to go?" He appears on the other side, fully dressed, in a suit that shows off the money he grew up around, that he wears like a glove, easily and lightly. He looks fucking hot as hell, frankly.

"Not quite," I reply. I ease the door open wider. "Could you help me?" I turn so my back is to him, my exposed skin tingling in the cool air.

He crosses the room to me, and takes the zipper in one hand, rests his other against my shoulder blades, his fingertips white hot on my skin. "Do you like the gown?" he murmurs, not moving the zipper yet. He looks past me, and I look up to find a mirror on the far side of the room, against a wardrobe. Looking at the two of us there, his hand at my lower back and another on my shoulder, we match. Two birds of a feather, getting dressed for some glamorous ball.

"It's not what I'd normally wear," I admit. I glance over my shoulder at him. He shakes his head, seems to recall himself, and zips up the dress.

But he doesn't take his hand away from my shoulder. And when I turn and place both palms on his chest, he doesn't step back from me. We both gaze at one another head-on now, entranced. "What about you?" I ask, leaning back, so my hair tumbles down my back, in the faint waves it always has when I've worn it up overnight. "Are you always the suit type?"

"I have to be," he answers.

"That doesn't really answer my question, does it?" I smile, tilt my head.

His eyes search mine, gaze as piercing and white-hot as ever. "No, I suppose it doesn't," he murmurs. But he doesn't answer the question. Instead, he lets his hand trail up my bare shoulder toward my neck. Just his fingertips, a barely there touch that makes the hair on the back of my neck stand up, and electricity fly through my veins. His fingertips pause when they reach my jawline, then curl along it until he's cupping my chin in his hand. "If you don't like the dress, you don't have to wear it." His voice comes out a breath, a whisper against my lips.

He's close, so close that our breath mingle, and all I can smell is his scent, delicious and sharp and distracting all at once. "Would you prefer if I took it off?" I ask, and I lift one eyebrow, playful, trying to lighten the suddenly heavy, stormy atmosphere.

"Very much so." And then his lips crash into mine again, and this time, I don't pretend I can possibly resist him. I wrap both arms around his neck and arch up against him, loving the sensation of his firm body against mine. I arch my hips and dig them against his, and his arm dips to circle my waist. He tightens his grip, crushes my body to his and picks me

up, just high enough to slide his feet under mine.
Then he walks us both, lips still crushed together, my
hips digging into his, and the hard press of his cock
against my belly—walks us backwards until my legs
bump into the bed.

We collapse across it, and he lands above me,
braced with one hand on the bed, the other still
tracing my jawline, down my neck, around to the back
of the gown to undo the zipper he just did.

I dig my hands into his back, pull him down
against me, hard and hungry. At the same time I lift
my legs to either side of his waist, arch up until I can
feel the outline of his cock against my soft stomach.
He feels huge against me, and I gasp a little as my
gown hikes up around my waist.

"God, you are exquisite," he murmurs against

my jawline, my neck. His lips move lower, even as his fingertips trail after the hem of my gown, hiking it farther up, until my legs are exposed, only my panties separating me from his suit pants. He arches against me, shifting lower, and I gasp as I feel the hard dig of his cock right over me.

He pauses and arches a brow at me, still poised above me. "Already wet for me, Dee?" He reaches a finger down and runs it over the outer edge of my panties, making me shiver with want. I'm already soaked through, and I know he can feel it.

In response, I slide a hand down his hips to trace the outline of his cock through his pants, pressing hard with my fingertips. "As wet for you as you are hard for me, Mr. Quint."

He flashes me a broad grin. "Aren't you the

naughty girl after all, Ms. Smith?" He leans back, and I gasp at the sudden loss of his heat, and the pressure of his fingers against my aching pussy, after so many days of thinking about him, fantasizing about this moment.

He leans back on the edge of the bed and watches me with those dark, hooded, unreadable eyes. "Take off your gown."

I stand up and slip off the shoulders, one at a time. I stand for a moment, holding it up, teasing. And then I let it drop to my ankles, and step out of it with a kick, smirking as I step toward him. "Do you like giving commands, Mr. Quint?"

"Only if you like to follow them, Ms. Smith." He tilts his head to one side, waiting.

In response, I spread my hands at my sides

and bow my head. "Tell me what you want."

He steps closer. Traces a hand over my hair, and then gently tilts my head back until I'm looking up at him once more. "You, beautiful." His eyes drink me in, taking their time. I'm wearing a lace slip of a bra, the only thing that fit under this gown, and my panties. That's it. Yet somehow, under his gaze, I don't feel exposed in a bad way.

I feel sexy. Brazen as hell. Maybe it's because of the way he takes me in, like he's loving every second of it, and he can't get enough.

"I want you every which way," he murmurs, and his lips brush my cheek, my neck, my collarbone. Dip down until he's kissing between my breasts, and his hands reach up to tweak my nipples, toy with them through my bra, and I get so hard so fast that I have to gasp. "But first, I want to enjoy the view." He steps back and smiles. "Lie down on the bed."

I do as I'm told.

"Spread your legs," he says, and I spread them wide. He hooks one thumb under my panties and tugs them down, in one swift motion. I gasp as the cool air of the hotel room brushes my bare pussy. My already soaking wet pussy. Then he climbs between my spread legs and runs his hands up my sides to my bra.

"Take it off," he says.

I lean forward to undo the clasp. Let it fall down my arms. He tosses it aside, and then he's over me again, his hands tracing the edges of my breasts. He leans down to kiss my chest, lick and suck underneath each breast, and then, one at a time, he swirls his tongue around my nipples, alternately thrashing them with his soft wet tongue and gently rolling them between his teeth, never biting hard enough to hurt, just enough to make me harder than a damn diamond.

I reach up to grab the clasp of his belt, unable to wait much longer. I whip that off, then tug at his shirt. I start undoing the buttons, but get frustrated halfway up, because he keeps nipping and sucking at my nipples, then dips lower, out of reach. He chuckles slightly against my belly, and his tongue flicks into my navel for a second, sending a shockwave of sensation all the way to my toes.

"Just tear it off, if you're so anxious," he murmurs against my stomach.

So I grab the shirt in both hands and rip. Buttons fly every which way. He laughs again, flashing me an appraising look.

"I didn't think you actually *would*," he's saying, but I don't give him time to pause and think about it. I grab his tie and yank him back down into a kiss, my legs wrapped around his waist now as I reach down with my other hand to grab for the waist of his pants.

He bites my lower lip as we part from the kiss, both of us breathless, and then he yanks on his own tie, undoes it, and tosses that aside after his shirt.

"God, Jasper." For a moment I pause, distracted by his now bare torso. Because God *damn* he is ripped. I knew he was cut from his build through the T-shirt, but now I can see every inch of his muscles, the perfect plane of his abs and the V-cut over his groin.

He smirks. "Like what you see?"

"Fuck yes," I whisper. I run my fingertips over it all, leaning up to kiss his pecs, his abs, and flick my tongue across his nipples.

He shudders above me, and I take that as encouragement and undo his pants button. "Dee…" he starts, but I don't listen. I yank the zipper down, and tug them over his hips. He lets them fall, and I push his boxers down after, eager.

His cock springs free, just inches from my face where I've arched up underneath him now, and it's all I can do to contain a pulse of white hot desire.

Desire… and concern.

Because he's huge. Thick and long, with a vein that stands out along one side, so irresistible that I can't help myself—I lean in to trace my tongue along it, and savor the way he gasps and digs his hands into my hair, tightening.

"Fuck, Dee," he groans through gritted teeth.

I run my tongue along him, from his base to his tip, exploring him as I marvel at his length, his thickness. I don't even know if I'll be able to fit him completely in my mouth, let alone my pussy. And yet, I've never been this wet for a guy, either. I've never felt like my clit was a lead weight between my legs, heavy and aching with desire.

Much as I'm enjoying myself, it's almost a relief when he gently pulls me back. "Not yet," he tells me, gaze on fire as he stares down at me. "I want to fuck you first."

My heart skips a beat at that.

He reaches for his pants, rifles in a pocket for a condom, and I hold out a hand for it, wordlessly. He places it in my palm, and I roll it down over his cock, savoring the velvety grip of him, the steel underneath.

"Not going to lie," he says, as he leans down along me, forcing me back down against the bed, his hands tracing my hips, my thighs. Down to part my legs and run one hand along my slit, a single fingertip delving between my folds to massage the wet warmth there, rocking back and forth, coating his finger in my juices. "I've been imagining this for a very long time, Dee." His gaze meets mine, white hot with naked lust. "I've wanted you since the moment I laid eyes on you."

I swallow hard around the fire that's flaring through my body. Distracting me. Making me catch flame, as he teases me again and again with that lone finger of his.

"I've fantasized about this. About making you scream my name."

I gaze up at him, dare a faint smile. "I've fantasized about screaming your name," I reply, and if anything, that only seems to make his stare hotter.

He adds a second finger, presses them against my entrance. Not quite entering me, not yet. "Why can't I get you out of my head, Dee?" he whispers, just before he slides those fingers inside me, an inch at a time, teasing into me.

My lips part in a silent gasp, eyes locked on his. I don't know what to say to that, don't know how to respond except to arch my hips up against him, grant him better access as he pushes his fingers deeper, deeper. When they reach their limit, he curls his fingertips inside me and draws them out again, dragging along my inner front wall, and I groan with delight, as the pads of his thick fingers graze over my G-spot.

"You are fucking sexy as hell," he murmurs, as he strokes his fingers out, and then gently glides them back in again. Back and forth. Working me up. Stoking the flames inside me. "And this tight, gorgeous little pussy of yours? Mmm." He grins and pauses to glance down. To watch as his fingers spread my lips and press into me. Then, without warning, he adds a third, and I gasp and buck beneath him. He starts to stroke his hand faster, harder. "I can't wait to spread those tight little lips with my fat cock. I can't wait to be inside you, fucking you…"

I start to rock my hips in time to his finger thrusts and his words, the pressure mounting. I reach down with one hand, unable to resist, and grab his cock, stroking him at the same time he strokes me. "I want… you to… fuck me," I manage, as much as I'm able to keep my head together in the midst of this firestorm.

"Ask me nicely." He leans down to kiss my lips, hard and hot, as he drives his fingers into me harder, faster.

I buck in time with him, and bite his lip as we break from the kiss, making us both gasp with want. "Fuck me, Jasper. Please, fuck me."

He grins and spreads my legs wide, and kneels between them. He draws his fingers out of my pussy, and it leaves me feeling exposed, empty, *wanting*.

Luckily not for long.

"Anything you want," he tells me. Then he

positions the tip of his cock at my entrance—he is *huge*, fuck—and slowly starts to press into me, one inch at a time.

I gasp faintly before he's even halfway into me. "God, Jasper…"

"Relax, Dee." His eyes find mine, hold on. "Trust me."

I loop my legs around his waist and try to do just that. Trust him. I relax, and he inches deeper into me, moving slowly, giving me time to adjust to his girth with each inch he presses into me. Finally, he's completely inside me, filling me, stuffing me deeper than I've ever been filled before.

"*Fuck* you feel good," I hiss.

"So do you." He leans down along me, and starts to draw back a little. I moan in protest at the loss. "Your tight little pussy feels so fucking incredible, Dee," he murmurs as he draws away.

But I don't have to miss him long. Another instant and he's back, thrusting deep into me again, a little bit faster this time, and I buck up against him to meet him, savoring the hot burn all throughout my body, the fire that it stokes in my belly. "Yes," I moan, head twisted to one side, lips parted. "Fuck me, Jasper."

"Not so fast." He tilts my head to one side, runs a hand through my hair and draws it back from my neck. Peppers little kisses all along the edge of my neck, up to the soft spot below my ear, where he nips me, just hard enough to make me gasp. "I want to enjoy this, Dee. Enjoy every…" He pulls out, slow, agonizingly slow. "Fucking." He starts to glide back in, slowly all over again. "Inch." He hits home, all the way inside me, and pulls back a little faster this time. "Of." Then he drives back in, faster still. "You."

With each thrust, my hips buck up against him, trying to grant him access, to let him take what he wants. Eventually, we find our rhythm, moving in sync, rocking faster and faster as his cock plunges into me, stretching my walls, making my pussy ache with want, with the pressure building inside.

Just when it starts to build to a peak, and my breath is coming in quick bursts, I reach down to grip his ass—his perfectly sculpted, hard as a rock, muscular ass, an ass I want to dig my fingers into and hold onto for dear life—and he stills inside me, all the way in, hips poised over me.

"Don't stop," I pant between breaths.

But he just grins down at me. "I told you, Dee. I want to enjoy the show." With that, he flips both of us, easily lifting me as he rolls onto his back, and swinging my leg around so I straddle his hips, all with his cock still buried inside me.

Before I can react, he reaches down to grab my hips in both hands and rocks me along him, pushing me up and pulling me back down to meet his bucking hips as he does. At this angle, his cock hits my G-spot with every thrust, driving me wild, running along my inner wall and making me wet and tight with want. I clench around him, crying out as the sensation starts to build toward a peak.

"Fuck yes, Dee. Come for me, come on my big cock." He keeps thrusting under me, controlling my movements, making me rise and fall over him, his hands so tight on my hips that it hurts, but I don't even care, because the pain is a good one, bone deep, like the ache I know I'll feel in my pussy tomorrow morning.

I arch my hips and ride him, as he fucks me from below, thrusting up into me hard and fast and deep, until I can't stand it anymore. The pressure has mounted too high, too fast to control. "I'm going to come," I gasp, breath coming short and fast. "Fuck. Jasper," I moan, almost there, so damn close. "I'm coming." I lose control of my vocal cords on the last word, crying aloud now, as the orgasm sweeps through me.

For a moment, all I can feel is pleasure, all I can see is white hot light. And he keeps going, keeps fucking me, pulling my hips down into his, crashing up against me, as his cock plunges deep inside my pussy again and again, making the orgasm last longer than I knew possible, and then, with another deep, guttural growl, he flips us again, landing on top of me to grab my shoulder with one hand, his other braced against the bed as he thrusts once, twice, a look of animal, desperate lust in his eyes.

He comes with a loud cry, deep inside me, and keeps thrusting, slower now, as the orgasm ripples through his body. I run my hands over his back, his chest, gripping him, pulling him down against me until our mouths find one another again, and his tongue lashes out at mine, and I get lost in that kiss, in his touch, wanting it to never end.

But it does, it has to. He draws back out of me, and a gasp of protest escapes my lips, unbidden. I feel empty without him, even though he just made me come.

I want him all over again, already, even now. What the hell is wrong with me?

As for Jasper, he's rolling away from me, drawing the condom off his cock. But when he glances at the clock beside the bed, he laughs a little, deep in his throat, as he leans over to throw away the condom.

"What is it?" I ask, craning my neck to see.

I catch a glimpse of are our ruined outfits— my gown a wrinkled mess on the floor, the satin not exactly up to snuff when it comes to us tumbling all over the bed in it. And on top of it his torn suit shirt, buttons surrounding it across the floor. My cheeks flare hot. I forgot about that.

What was wrong with me?

"I don't think we're going to make our dinner reservations," he says, a smirk on his so damn kissable lips.

I glance past him then, and at the clock this time. Wow. When did it get so late? My cheeks warm. "Whoops."

He grins, apparently not disappointed in the least. "Whoops indeed." Then he leans back in to kiss me once more, slow and steady. "That's all right. We'll call room service." He pauses and smiles down at me, eyes hot again with want. Same as me. He wants me again too. "But only after I've had my fill of you first…"

CHAPTER SEVEN

Jasper

God, this woman. I cannot get enough of her.

Even now, even right after fucking her, when most women usually start to lose their shine for me—what can I say?—she still retains it. All I want to do is fuck her again right now, but that will have to wait, at least a little while.

Luckily, there's still plenty I can do to have my fill of her in the meantime.

I catch her ankles and drag her to the edge of the bed, where I spread her knees and kneel between them. From this angle, looking up at her over the plane of her stomach and the mounds of her breasts, I can't say I've ever seen a sexier woman. I love every inch of her, from her pert nipples to her broad hips, which felt perfect with my hands wrapped tight around them as I thrust into her.

And her pussy...

I spread her lips with two fingers and breathe in her scent, sharper here than ever, yet still the same, still *her* at its essence.

"Jasper," she moans, and my name in her mouth, on her lips, drives me crazier than anything else tonight.

I slip my tongue between her lips and trace the length of her slit with the tip. *Fuck.* "You taste amazing," I breathe, breath hot against her skin, before I lean in to lick her again, slower, longer, trailing the flat of my tongue between her lips and all the way up and over her clit.

She gasps, her clit no doubt already sensitive from her first orgasm, and I flatten a palm against her stomach, pin her against the bed as I bend down to taste her better, lick every inch of her. I run my tongue along her slit, back and forth, a few times, tasting each edge of her lips, until finally, I circle the narrowed tip of my tongue around her entrance, savoring her flavor, the way she gasps and writhes on the bed in anticipation.

"Jasper, please," she moans.

I pause, grinning at her impatience. "Please what, Dee?" My eyes flash when they catch hers.

She swallows hard, wets her lips with a flick of her tongue before she speaks. "Please, make me come again."

"And how do you want me to do that, Dee?" I ask, playful, though I make sure to blow hot air along her slit as I speak, making her shiver and twist in anticipation.

"I want... you to eat me out." She catches my eye, holds it. "I want your tongue inside my pussy. I want you to lick my clit until I—"

She doesn't finish that sentence, because I take the chance to plunge my tongue into her pussy. She moans aloud, and her hips buck up to meet me, so her whole pussy is spread against my mouth, there for the taking. I press my tongue as deep into her as I can and draw it back out, slow and hard, curled to rub along her G-spot as I do. She cries out faintly when I press it, and I circle back, running the tip of my

189

tongue over that spot again and again as she bucks beneath me, until I draw my tongue back out of her pussy with a soft, wet smack, and press her back down against the bed.

I pin her there with one hand and run my tongue around her clit, teasing the edges, while my other hand presses inside her. I curl a finger in her pussy, stroke it along her walls, as I tongue her clit with the flat of my tongue, not too hard, not enough to send her overboard, with how sensitive she is right now.

Each time, she gasps and bucks against me and calls my name, begs me to never stop.

I don't want to, either. I want to go on tasting her and driving her wild for as long as I can. I love this, love her taste, love driving her so wild she forgets where she is, what she's doing. I want to make her wild like this every night.

I want to make her *mine*.

Finally, when I think she's had enough, I pull back and tongue her again, slow and steady now, until she cries out, her whole body shaking, and her pussy tightening around my finger still deep inside her. She convulses, writhes, but I don't stop, not yet. I keep going, slide my finger out of her pussy and replace it with my tongue again, licking her deep and pointed, right on the right spot, until she comes a second time, her breath gasping, pussy twitching around me.

Finally, I draw back, my lips and chin wet with her juices, and kiss my way back up her stomach, her breasts—pausing to give those some attention, first one and then the other, savoring the perfect handful size of them and the way her nipples harden at my touch, so sensitive, so reactive. Then I trail up farther, kissing her neck, her jawline, finally her mouth, where she can taste herself on my lips. I swirl my tongue around hers, dance with her, as she arches up against me, still hungry, still wanting.

Which is good. I'm not done with her yet.

We part from the kiss, and I smirk down at her. "How do you taste on my mouth?" I ask. "Because if you ask me, I think you taste fucking incredible."

"Mm. I'd say you taste better," she replies, with a quick glance at my groin, and my cock throbs, already semi-hard again from my mouth against her wet pussy, and growing harder by the second. Especially now that she's looking at it, reminding me of the first thing she did the moment my pants dropped—trailing her tongue along my length. "But I didn't get a good enough taste last time," she says. "So I can't be sure yet."

"Well then." I lean back on the bed, arms above my head, and grin at her. "Feel free to have a second taste, for comparison's sake."

She grins back at me, then leans down to kiss my neck. My chest. My abs, tracing her tongue over the grooves of my muscles. "Mm... All right," she says, eyes alight with mischief. "But only for comparison's sake."

"Of course," I agree, smirking.

By the time she reaches my cock, I'm fully hard again, solid as a rock, in the way only she's been able to make me do so fast again, so soon after a fuck like that. But then, everything with Dee has been surprising from start to finish. Surprisingly easy, surprisingly sexy. Surprisingly *hot as hell* in the bedroom.

All I want to do is spend forever in this room, figuring out just how surprising we can make things.

She swirls her tongue around the tip of my cock, teasing me, tasting me, and I can tell by the way she eyes me that she's nervous about my size.

"Take it slow," I tell her, but as soon as the words have left my mouth, she defies them, the way only Dee seems to constantly be able to do.

She leans down and wraps her lips around me, sudden and swift, the pillows of her curved lips looking and feeling fucking amazing wrapped around my smooth cock. She inches her head down, and I reach down with both hands to run them through her soft, golden curls. I tighten my grip, enjoy the view of her breasts dangling underneath her as she bends over me, dipping her head down. Before I realize it, I'm clenching her hair in fists, but she only smiles up at me, eyes on fire with desire. Her tongue flicks along my underside, strong and targeted, flicking over the vein there, tracing its length and driving me wild, as she eases herself farther down my cock.

I can feel when she thinks she's done, when she pauses, unsure of herself, whether she can go any farther.

"Relax," I tell her, my voice low. And then I pull her head down a little farther, hair still wrapped in my fists. "If you want me to stop, just tap my leg," I say, but instead, she tightens her grip on me, both hands clenched tight around my thighs like all she wants to do is devour me whole and take home the blue ribbon for best blow job.

I have to say, she's well on the way toward earning that.

I feel the tip of my cock touch the back of her throat, and I expect her to tap my leg now, surrender, but she pulls herself forward, deeper, and I pull her down against me in response, feel her throat relax and loosen to accommodate an inch of my cock, before she pulls back again, half a second later.

"Fuck, Dee," I murmur, as she slides back up my length, triumph in her gaze now. "You are fucking phenomenal at this…"

She slides right back down, only a low murmur in the back of her throat in response. A murmur that sends a shockwave through my body, as the hum transmits itself from her mouth and around my cock. She laughs when my cock tenses and jumps between her lips, and then she keeps humming, as she starts to rock back and forth, and adds her tongue in to the mix.

"Your mouth is almost as hot and wet as your pussy," I comment with a smirk.

With each thrust that she takes me into her throat, I feel my fists tightening in her hair, my muscles tensing as I rise, faster and faster, toward another peak. Before long, I'm fucking her face in earnest, drawing her down against me with abandon, unable to control myself, wild with lust. And she loves it, still making throaty moans in the back of her throat that only add to the tension, and swirling her tongue around my base.

"You like that?" I murmur, low in my throat, as I pull her against me another time. "You like when I fuck your throat? You like feeling my cock in your mouth?"

She murmurs an assertive, and I suck in a gasp through clenched teeth at the vibrations again.

But it's when she reaches between my legs with both hands to grasp my balls, gently tugging on them, toying with them as she continues to suck me into her throat, that's when I really have to brace myself.

"Fuck, Dee, I'm getting close."

She bobs her head faster, and I thrust up against her, forgetting about everything but her lips, her mouth, her perfect fucking body, those breasts of her swaying with every thrust.

"I'm going to come."

She tightens her lips, lashes her tongue against me.

"I'm gonna come... in your... throat," I groan, teeth gritted.

She swallows around me in anticipation, and that does it. I grab her face, pull her against me as the wave hits. I feel my cum shoot down her throat, and she swallows again, again. *Fuck this girl is incredible.* Finally, when the last pulses of my cum have gone, I release her, draw back enough for her to let go of my cock, lean back, and then bend down to flick her tongue over my length, cleaning up every last drop, any she might have missed, and licking her lips, savoring it.

"Fuck, Dee," I manage.

She just grins at me, like she knows exactly what she's doing to me.

I reach up to grab her and pull her down along me, then roll her over beside me. This time when I kiss her, it's me I taste, mingled with the taste of her mouth, her lips. The whole room smells like sex and our sweat, and I swear there's never been a better scent in the world.

I don't know what the hell I'm getting into here. All I know is, I don't want out of it anytime soon…

****

I wake up to the blare of an alarm clock,

200

dazed, my head swimming. It takes me a moment to register the warm body in my arms, and another moment to remember last night. Everything.

I squint past Dee's mess of wavy hair toward the distant clock. 9:55AM. Not that we had anything to do today, really, except drive back home sometime in the afternoon. But normally I'm always up by 8 at the latest, never one for sleeping in.

I guess that changes when I'm up late. Up all night, really, being distracted as hell by the gorgeous creature dozing in my arms, apparently undisturbed by the alarm clock. I reach out with my foot and try to turn it off without moving her, but I miss, and there's a crash as it clatters onto the hotel floor.

I wince and glance at Dee, but she hasn't even stirred. Deep sleeper, I guess. Gently, I disentangle myself from her and ease out of bed. Then I crouch on the floor and slap the alarm clock off, and put it back on the nightstand.

By the time I sit up again, Dee is mumbling in her sleep, rolling over, and then blinking at me, bleary-eyed. She hesitates, a faint crease appearing between her brows, as if she's having the same issue I did waking up this morning—a brief short-circuit before we remember everything that happened last night.

Then she smiles, and relief floods through me. "What are you doing down there?" She reaches out and nudges me with a toe. "Weirdo."

I climb back into bed. "Just saving us from a rude awakening." I bend down to kiss her bare shoulder, and then shift the covers to expose her waist, as I roll her beneath me and kiss her collarbone next, then the gentle slope of her chest leading down between her breasts, to the flat little area between them both. I flick my tongue along there as she sighs under her breath.

"Still not satisfied after last night?" she asks, a smirk on her face.

"Hmm. No, actually." I tilt my chin up to rest on her chest and grin up at her. "Oddly, as satisfying as last night *was*, I don't think I'll ever be satisfied with my fill of you."

The words hang in their air between us for a moment, full of other unspoken things. Comments I know she must be tempted to make, such as ones about the business side of our situation, or complications.

But to my surprise, she doesn't voice any of those this time. She just reaches down with both hands to pull me back up over her, until I'm above her, our noses touching, face-to-face. "I know that feeling," she whispers. Then our mouths collide, and I run my hands down her sides to those curvy hips of hers that I love, running my hands around the edges to grip her ass beneath me, and we both forget what we were just talking about, because *fuck* that feels good.

I can't resist her any longer. I spread her legs with one hand and find her already wet and wanting, arching up against my hand like the hungry, greedy girl she is, and that drives me wild. But as I start to stroke along her slit, something catches my eye. A glint from the side table.

I cast a sideways glance at it, and feel a grin spread across my face. With a nod toward the table, I catch her eye. "Put your ring on, Mrs. Quint."

She stills beneath me, but only for a second. From the way her breath hitches, I can tell she likes the idea as much as I do, even if she doesn't want to admit it. She hesitates a moment, then reaches across beneath me, her movement making her thighs brush against my bare cock, and sending an aching thrill through my body. She catches the ring, and slides it onto her left hand. "You mean this ring, Mr. Quint?"

"The one I gave you when I asked you to be my wife, yes." I trace my cock along her inner thigh, up one side and down the other, my hand still working along her slit, spreading her pussy lips, exploring her. Savoring the slickness of the juices that spill out, showing that she's just as eager for me as I am for her.

"Does that get you hard, Mr. Quint?" She arches a brow, then reaches down to grasp my cock between both hands, stroking my length, her hands tightening just enough to make me groan between my teeth. "Do you like thinking about making me your wife?"

I gaze down at her from beneath hooded eyes. "I like thinking about claiming you for my own, wife. I like knowing you belong to me." I catch her hands, and gently draw them off my cock. It takes effort to stop her, because her stroking felt good, *really fucking good*, but I want to guide this one. So I draw her hands up over her head and gently lean forward until she's pinned beneath me, hands above her head, body stretched out long and lithe and waiting for me to do whatever I want to her.

And I want to do so damn much.

I switch hands, so I'm holding both of hers in one of mine—her wrists are so small that even with both her hands clasped in mine, she's easy to pin in place. I grin down at her, and she smiles right back, white-hot lust in her eyes. I love the look she gets when she's like this—just as hungry for me as I am for her.

"Do you belong to me, Mrs. Quint?" At this, I stroke my finger up to her clit and circle it lightly with my thumb, pressing just hard enough to elicit a gasp of satisfaction from her.

"I do." Her eyes catch mine, full of spark, full of mischief. "Do you belong to me, Mr. Quint?" she asks, and she arches her back, then, writhes beneath me as I continue to circle her clit, bringing her closer and closer to her climax. At the same time, she lifts her hips off the bed, makes sure that those long, smooth thighs of hers graze along my bare cock, teasing, taunting.

I groan in the back of my throat, a guttural sound, hidden behind clenched teeth. "Oh, I do, Mrs. Quint. I really do." I lean down then to kiss her neck, taste the sweat that pools against her clavicle, as I stroke my thumb faster, and slide my middle finger inside her soaking wet pussy at the same time. I stroke her from the inside and out, pinching her, just hard enough to drive her wild. Only when I'm good and ready do I lean back and smile down at her, prepared for the show.

"You can come for me now, Mrs. Quint," I whisper, and she doesn't waste any time.

Her voice rises in gasps as she lifts her hips, twists and moans beneath me. She calls out my name when her climax hits, but I keep my finger inside her, add a second one, continue to stroke her until she's right there at the edge again, gasping "Don't stop, don't ever stop."

I lean down to catch her mouth in mine for her second orgasm, and she moans into my mouth as I kiss her, hard and long and deep, tasting her desire, savoring the feel of her body shivering with pleasure underneath mine.

Finally, when she's soaked and breathing hard, I reach past her with my free hand to grab a condom, tearing it from the foil and rolling it down my cock in a single, practiced motion.

"Fuck me, Mr. Quint," she gasps, spreading her knees wide. "Fuck me now." I lie between them, and she wraps her legs around my waist, granting me easy access to her.

I press the tip of my cock against the entrance of her pussy and smile down at her, gaze hooded. "Ask me nicely, Mrs. Quint." I circle the tip of my cock around her, sliding back and forth along her slit, coating myself in her juices, driving her wild.

She twists beneath me, impatient, and I'm loving it. Loving that I drive her as crazy as she drives me. "Please," she finally breathes, voice low and breathy. "Please fuck me."

I smile a little. Press my tip into her, just half an inch, just enough to make her cry out again, louder.

"Please fuck me, Mr. Quint."

This time I really drive myself home, pressing into her fully in one thrust, and her head falls back, her neck arching as she groans.

I fucking love her pussy. The way she tightens around me like a glove, squeezing me so hard. And yet when I draw back, I glide easily within her, because she's so fucking wet for me. "Your pussy is fucking perfect, do you know that, Mrs. Quint?" I slide out to the very edge of her, and then thrust forward again, until the spongy tip of my cock hits home within her, filling her completely, stuffing her full of my thick cock. Not all women have been able to handle me—sometimes I have to tread carefully, lightly. But not Dee.

211

She drives me as well as she drives my cars.

"I love watching you writhe on my big cock." I pull back, thrust again, and she drives her hips up to meet mine, pushing me more fully home. "I love feeling how full I make you."

"So fucking full." Her eyelids flutter, almost close, as I start to rock faster, build up a rhythm. "Fuck, Jasper, don't stop, fill me up, fucking fill me up."

I pull her legs up, push them up over my shoulders so she's spread beneath me on the bed, and grasp her hips in both hands, powering home into her with each drive. I tilt my hips to drag my cock along the front wall of her pussy, my tip pressing into her with each thrust. She's already sensitive from me stroking her to orgasm twice, and it doesn't take long before another starts to build in her.

She cries aloud when it hits, and I cannot get enough of this sight.

That's the woman I'm going to marry, a hazy, sex-dazed part of my brain thinks as I gaze down at her, prone before me, breasts shaking each time I thrust inside her, my balls slapping against her ass. *She's mine.*

Of course it's all for show. All play-acting. Just a game that makes it hotter than hell when we fuck. But a little part of my brain starts to think, would it be so bad if this weren't for show after all?

Because as much as I love watching her eyes flutter half-closed and her lips part and her face flush with heat and lust as she comes for me, comes on my big thick cock, her pussy clenching around me like a hand fisting my cock, as much as I love the sex... I

213

also fucking love that diamond flashing on her finger, and the way she was looking at me from beneath those lowered eyelashes of hers.

Husband and wife. It has a fucking hot ring to it, doesn't it?

I've never felt that way before. Not about a woman I've fucked, not about any woman I've dated. But with her, I can start to really, truly picture it for the first time.

I finish inside her with a growl, and we both collapse to the bed, sweaty, the sheets tangled around us, slick from sex and desire and wanting. I pull her to me for another long, deep kiss, and all I want to do is stay in this bed all day. Keep fucking her, keep driving her wild. I never want to get back in the car that's waiting for us downstairs. I never want to go home.

Not without her.

I am so fucking screwed.

CHAPTER EIGHT

Dee

We were supposed to arrive back from our weekend getaway early on Sunday morning. Originally we'd planned to come back in the afternoon and swing by the office, in case anybody was still around over the weekend working late hours who might be able to play witness to our rendezvous.

But then Saturday night happened. And then Sunday morning happened. And then neither of us wanted to get out of bed, much less drive all the way back just to go to work and pretend we're pretending to be a couple, when in reality... I think maybe something else is happening.

I don't know. All I know is we ordered room service again Sunday, ate brunch naked on the bed, with several platters of room service between us, polishing off waffles with decadent piles of cream and strawberries in between taking plentiful helpings of that cream and those strawberries and spreading them across each other's bodies. Then eating the strawberries, one by one, him sometimes foregoing the strawberries altogether to concentrate on trailing his tongue around my nipples instead, making them hard as rocks before he finally relents with a grin.

He knows exactly how wild he drives me, damn him.

By the time the front desk called to remind us of the checkout time, we were so distracted by that

217

Jasper told them to book us for another night.

"But—" I started to protest, thinking about work, but he shushed me.

"We'll head back first thing in the morning. You'll be there in time to meet with the other interns."

The other interns. The other interns who spent all last week casting side-eye at me and whispering about how I skipped orientation for a private tour with Jasper Quint instead. The ones who didn't bother to hide their slack-jawed shock when I left the office with Jasper just after noon on Friday, after he wrote to my supervisor to notify her of a business need.

Not going to lie, I'm a little nervous about returning now, like this, in the same clothes I left work in on Friday, speeding up to the door with Jasper in his father's vintage car.

Not to mention, I have about a million unread messages from Melissa on my phone.

So, did it happen? was the first one on the docket. The whole lead-up to this weekend getaway, she'd teased me that Jasper wanted to get in my pants. I kept denying it, kept saying we were keeping things strictly business. Now...

My stomach churns.

"You okay?" Jasper casts me a sideways look from his side of the car. He's driving this morning, so I can apply a little bit of makeup, at least enough to look semi-presentable in an attempt to pretend I have a real job here.

I want to work hard in this internship. I want

to be taken seriously. But I didn't really think about that side of things when I signed on for this extra position—the Mrs. One: I didn't think about what the other people at the company would say or think about me, the new girl who rolled into the office and straight into Jasper's bed.

And normally I'd be able to brush it off, since this is all for show anyway, all pretend, the wedding, all of it…

Except now I'm not so sure it is, anymore.

I mean, the wedding is fake. The ring is fake. Our engagement, that side of things, fake. But Saturday night? Sunday morning? Hell, even this morning, when Jasper caught me in the shower and pinned me against the wall, kneeling between my legs to eat me out one last time, soapy water cascading down my body as my cries of pleasure echoed in the marble tiled bathroom?

That was real. Sharing a bad was real. And I'm worried that there might be more to this thing than just sex. Because—don't get me wrong, the sex is fucking phenomenal, and I regret none of it... But the way he stared into my eyes this morning, like a man lost at sea. The way I stared back, like a woman reaching out to him for a lifeline...

He scares me. *This* scares me. I didn't expect it, didn't see it coming. Never in a million years would I have guessed I could form a connection this deep with somebody, let alone somebody like Jasper. But we stayed up late into the night last talking about our families—I shared stories about my parents, and for once, telling those stories didn't make me sad or send me right back into the depression I first fell into when they passed. Instead it made me happy, because it made Jasper so obviously happy to hear those stories.

And he shared right back. He told me about his and his father's close relationship, about how much he loves working with his dad at the company. He talked about his cousins, the huge family that awaits us at the reunion in Greece. He lit up when he talked about how many cousins he has, and about how many little kids in the extended family her gets to spoil. He has no nieces and nephews, since he has no siblings, but his cousins are like siblings to him, from the sound of it, and he treats their children the same way I'd spoil any nieces or nephews if I had some.

"I'm fine," I tell him now, gaze fixed out the window of the car.

His mouth tightens into a thin line, like he doesn't believe me. But to his credit, he doesn't press me. He just stares out the window ahead and steers us up toward the work lot.

I watch the building approach, apprehension growing in my stomach. The glares and sideways mutters I heard spoken about me last week were already bad. I can't imagine how much worse they'll be now, when I walk in with this *rock* on my finger. I didn't think about this—we need our relationship to be visible so his father can see it, so Jasper's plan to win his inheritance can play out. But other people will see it too. And those people will be judging my part in this, not just Jasper's.

I suck in a deep breath, at the same moment that Jasper asks, "Are you ready for this?"

I let out my breath in a gust of laughter. "I was just about to ask you the same thing." I glance at him, then hold up the rock between us. It flashes in the sunlight. It's gaudier than the other ring I liked, way over the top. But then again, this is Jasper Quint we're talking about. Of course he went for the over-the-top ring. "How much of a bomb am I going to set off when I walk into the building wearing this today?" I ask.

"Well, Caroline might try to claw your eyes out," he admits, mouth twisted in a wry expression.

"You heart-breaker," I tease.

He sighs. "I was upfront at the start that there would be no hearts involved."

"I know how that goes." I lean back in my seat, twisting the belt in one hand.

"Yes, I'd imagine little Ms. I've Never Fallen in Love has broken her fair share of hearts in time. No?"

Now it's my turn to blush, and turn my head away. "Only one." Way back when. A classmate who I wanted as a friend with benefits. Turns out he wanted more, but I couldn't offer it. "Like you said. I was upfront at the start. But sometimes people think they'll be okay with an idea, and then the reality turns out to be very different."

"I can imagine how that happens with you." When I turn back to him, as he glides into a parking lot out behind the office, his eyes have gone dark and serious once more. "I'll bet nobody's quite able to forget about you, Dee. Not if they really get to know you well."

My head is still spinning from those words, and his expression as he says them, when he steps out of the car. I reach for my own door handle, but before I can get to it, he's beaten me to it, pulling open the door for me like he's his own valet. I smirk at him as I climb from the car. "I thought you said we wealthy people were supposed to let valets do that," I point out, recalling his lesson at the hotel.

He laughs. "Just teasing you, Dee. I'm not *that* pompous."

I hear a scoff, a little ways off, and turn just in time to catch a drift of blonde hair passing into the office from the rear doors, near the parking lot. The receptionist he just mentioned. Caroline.

Damn.

I shake my head and try to forget about her as

I grab my luggage from Jasper and wheel it after him into the building. We stash it in his office for now, and then, in the middle of the lobby, he pauses to wrap one arm around my waist and give me a very long, very public parting kiss, before I head for the start of my day.

My cheeks are flushed, my head ringing, and I catch Caroline glaring at me over the top of her computer monitor, eyes narrowed into pinpricks.

I try to catch my breath, but between racing to the staff meeting, arriving late, and being faced with another round of glares upon entry, it's hard to do. I sit in the back of the room, heart still racing, and listen to what the supervisor is saying. Or try to, anyway. Last week, we spent most of our time learning the ropes—what papers to file where, who'd need help with which projects. This week, though, we'll be expected to take a little more initiative in deciding where we want to work for the first couple weeks of the internship. The supervisor asks us who wants to help out in the design room.

My hand shoots into the air at once. Unfortunately, so do about five other people's in the room.

And the supervisor passes me over, pointing them out one after the other.

I lower my hand into my lap, disappointment stinging a little bit, but I ignore it and wait for another opportunity. The next shift is handed out—some people sent to assist engineering, others to the test track. Finally, only me and three other girls are left in the room, alone with the supervisor who peers over his clipboard and glances at me, then the others, then back to his assignments. "You four are going to head down to accounting for this rotation."

My stomach sinks into the floor.

Accounting? I didn't come here to learn how to balance budgets. My forehead creases in disappointment. But hey, the rotations change every couple of weeks. Just because I don't get to work in design or something fun right away doesn't mean I won't get my chance eventually. I just have to do well at this, prove myself—prove that I'm more than just Jasper's current gold-digging fiancée—and then I'll have my shot.

Maybe a boring assignment is for the best anyway, when I have so much extra work on the side.

Work. Part of me laughs to think of our

agreement that way now. It may have started out as an on-paper agreement, but it certainly doesn't feel that way anymore. Not after tasting his kisses, feeling his huge cock buried inside me. Not after watching the way his face goes slack and his eyes focused on me, crying out my name when he finishes deep in me.

"—Says she heard them talking in the parking lot," one of the girls ahead of me on my way out the door is whispering. "She was berating him for opening her car door. She said they should let the valets do that."

"Oh, my God. How pompous can you get?" another hisses.

"Shh." The third one elbows the other two, and all three turn plastic-fake grins on, just in time for me to emerge from the office.

My face turns beet-red. But I can imagine who told them that. *Caroline.* My heart sinks, remembering my lighthearted teasing of Jasper. I guess from the outside that might have sounded douchey... But I didn't mean it that way. Surely Caroline must have heard the way I said it, how we were joking.

I think about what Jasper told me, about them hooking up once years ago. Is that why she hates me now?

Is that why these other girls are casting sideways glances at the rock on my finger, and tittering and elbowing one another, as though I can't see them, as though I'm not standing right here?

"So, accounting," I say, in an attempt to stave off any more banter. "Pretty boring assignment, huh?"

"I'll find anything we're assigned to do here fascinating, I'm sure," one girl replies with a turn of her shoulder.

Another offers me an apologetic smile—the one who told the other two to shush when I approached—but she, too, turns away to follow the others down the hall.

"*Some* of us have to work for our positions, after all," the first girl who spoke mutters as we march through the corridors.

I drop my head, clench my fists inside my pockets where no one will be able to see them. Where no one will be able to see the ring, either. How much more of this can I handle?

This isn't forever, I remind myself. I just need to

keep my head down, work hard, and get a good recommendation from Jasper. Then move on, go to school, get a better job, somewhere I won't immediately be branded as the gold-digger sleeping with the boss.

But they're right, aren't they? says out the little nagging voice at the back of my head. *That's exactly what you're doing, isn't it?*

So I should be punished for it? I argue back mentally. These girls don't know me or Jasper. What if it was true love?

What if it is?

I shove that feeling down into the pit of my stomach. There it can grow, turn to poison, sicken me from the inside out. But I refuse to even think it. Not when this has already blown up into a bigger, more complicated mess than I ever anticipated.

What have I gotten myself into?

The moment I get a minute to myself, I slip into the bathroom to text Melissa back. I tell her the whole story—the hookup, the mornings after. The return to the office, and the glares I'm getting from just about everyone else here.

Okay, well firstly, screw those gossipers, she replies, which makes me almost smile. *Let she who is without sin cast the first stone, or whatever, if we're going Biblical. But more importantly—how was it???*

Amazing, is the only thing I can think to reply. Because it was. *He* was, more than I'd ever expected. *But I don't know if it's worth all this fall-out,* I add quickly. *I should be keeping my eye on my professional goals right now.*

Girl, you do. You're a workaholic, you love cars—I

have exactly zero doubts that you're pulling your weight at this internship. Who cares what those other girls think? They don't know the full story. All that matters if that you're enjoying yourself. And that hunky-as-hell husband of yours.

She adds a whole slew of winking faces, and I snort. This time, my smile is almost fully real. *Thanks. I'll try and remember that.* But I can't shake the nagging sensation that maybe, for once in our years-long friendship, Melissa might be wrong. Because if this is how other girls in my own office are judging me for the side-gig I've accepted, how will it look once the wider world learns I'm supposed to marry Jasper Quint?

****

"How was your day?" Jasper meets me in the

235

lobby with a bouquet of flowers and a huge, shit-eating grin on his face. But his expression dips a little when I don't return it.

"Not bad," I say, accepting the flowers with a forced smile. I lean up to kiss his cheek.

"Uh uh." He leans away. "Not buying it. What happened?"

"Nothing happened." My cheeks turn bright red, not for the first time throughout this long, long day of pretending I didn't overhear all the stuff the other girls were saying while we worked through a huge stack of overdue invoices down in accounting, inputting them into the computer, making up spreadsheets… "I just got put into accounting for my first rotation. It's fine, just…"

"A lot of busywork?" Jasper nods, knowingly,

to my surprise. "Been there. My dad started me in accounting for the first two years I worked here. Wouldn't let me advance into any of the fun stuff until I got a grasp on how the financial side of the business worked." He smiles a little wryly.

"Well. Two years? I certainly can't complain about two weeks then." I laugh. But my worried expression remains, and after a beat, he rests a hand on the small of my back and shoots a glance over my head toward the receptionist's desk on the far end of the lobby.

Caroline is not so subtly glaring daggers at us over her computer screen.

"Did anything else happen?" he asks. "Did Caroline try and mess with your head? She's done that before, to another girl I had a fling with down in engineering..."

"How many girls here have you had flings with?" I roll my eyes and elbow his side. "Sounds like you should be getting the flak around here, not me."

"You're getting flak?" A worried crease appears between his brows.

"No, I mean... That's not..." I shake my head. "It's fine." The last thing I want to do is stir up more trouble, or get anyone a bad name with higher-up management just because they're spreading perfectly true gossip about me.

"What's going on? Talk to me, Dee."

"It's just hard, you know?" I draw my left hand out of my pocket for what feels like the first time in hours and let the ring catch the overhead lights as we stride through the lobby, out toward

Jasper's car. "I feel like I just painted a target on my back. Everyone knows who I am now, and not for anything I've done, but just because I'm *Jasper's Quint's out-of-nowhere fiancée*."

He laughs for a second. "That sounds like the bad title of a romance novel." Then he sobers, after a glance at my face. "No, I understand. I have to admit, I didn't really think about this side of things when we made our, ah…" He waits until we clear the doors and reach the empty parking lot, and are halfway to his car before he speaks again. "This arrangement." He opens the door for me like usual, and I smile up at him as I climb into the passenger side seat.

"It's okay, really. I'll get used to it."

"If you'd prefer, you don't have to work with the other interns," he says, once he's in the driver's seat. "I can have you moved to another area of the company—"

"Oh, no. That would only make it worse." I wince, just imagining the rumors that would fly then. *She's sleeping with him so he'll play favorites and give her whatever assignment she wants.* "Really, Jasper. I have to handle this fall-out from our bargain. I'll deal with it, okay?" I rest my hand over his on the gearshift. "Now, do you mind dropping me off at home?"

"I can." His gaze drifts to me. Holds mine. "Or we could go back to my condo."

My heart skips a beat. "Are you sure?" I ask. Not what I meant to say. What I meant to say was *Thanks but I need to go home first. I have to change, I need to drop off my luggage...* Instead, I find myself leaning across the console toward him, smiling, as he mirrors me and leans in too.

"Absolutely," he murmurs. Then our lips meet, and I sink into his kiss, and I forget about it all. The worries. The fear about what people are saying. Who cares about any of that?

He slides one hand around my waist, draws me toward him, until I'm practically half on the gear shift, and his hand runs up the front of my dress, caressing my bra, teasing my nipple, taunting me with what's awaiting me back at his condo. Back when we're alone again, just the two of us, no pressure from anybody else to be or say or do what they find appropriate.

I have what I need right here, I think, and sink into his kiss.

CHAPTER NINE

Jasper

Dee and I fall into a rhythm. Nights at my place—long nights that I curse for ending. Nights when I take her every way I want her, in every room my the condo. I fuck her against the front door one night, unable to wait a second longer because the pencil skirt she's wearing is driving me wild. I hike it up around her hips, pick her up and brace her body with mine, her legs wrapped around my waist as I fuck her against the wood paneling, her hands digging into my shoulders, the nails leaving half-moons on my shoulders that make me smile when I see them morning.

Another night I fuck her on the kitchen counter, distracted halfway through us attempting to cook dinner together. We burn the rice, and wind up ordering delivery instead. While we're waiting on that, I bend her over the arm of the couch, thrust deep into her, again and again until we're both breathless and she's screaming my name at the top of her lungs.

The third night we come home together, my neighbor issues a noise complaint. In response, we make sure to fuck on the floor right above his bedroom, her with the pair of high heels she wore to work still on, so they clatter against the floor for extra sound effects.

I don't know what's gotten into me. I've never been like this before, never felt like this about a woman. I sext her all day long, asking for selfies, and when she finally caves in on Friday and sneaks into the ladies' room to send me a snapshot of the panties she's wearing, barely covering the lines of her clean-shaven pussy, I have to cancel an afternoon meeting to lock myself in my private office bathroom and jerk off, my hand tightly fisted around my cock, eyes squeezed tight shut as I picture her perfect tits, the way her ass bounces when I fuck her on all fours.

The office, of course, is a rumor mill on steroids. Caroline has stopped speaking to me altogether, passing me my mail with a cold, blank stare. Finally. If only I knew this was all I needed to do in order to get her to stop pining after me.

But I do feel bad about the effect all these rumors are having on Dee. She tries to hide it, tries to cover up the way it upsets her, but I can read it on her face at dinner, anytime I ask her about her day, about the internship. She blames it all on accounting, but I know better. I just feel so helpless. She asked me not to reassign her, not to play favorites, and I get what she means, that would look worse. But surely there has to be something I can do, some way to make up for this mess I've stuck her in.

After all, it's not like she really strode in here trying to play gold-digger. Greg and I picked her out of a stack of applicants because we knew she'd be the least likely candidate to win my father's affections. We knew whispers about a broke girl seducing me this fast would raise red flags everywhere. We molded her into this shape, and now she's the one being blamed for it.

It's not fair.

But then, I never expected Dee to be… well, *Dee*. I never expected to meet a woman like her, a woman I can discuss every topic that pops into my mind with, from car specs to baseball, which it turns out we're both obsessed with, to any old topic I stumble across in the morning news or hear on the radio. She's smart, she's funny, she's well-versed in pop culture. She's the total package. Wife material, as some might say.

Turns out that in fake marriages, I know how to pick 'em. But what happens when that fake marriage is beginning to feel *far* too real for me? What happens when our business arrangement runs out, and I don't want it to end?

These are the thoughts running through my

head when I run into Greg on my way into work the Monday before our reunion. We fly to Greece two days from now, and all I can think about is Dee, and what's going to happen once we get to the other side of this reunion. What's going to become of the nights we steal together, the mornings we have before we come into the office. All the thousand little in-between moments, stolen glances over the water cooler, winks while we wait in separate cafeteria lines at work. Feeling my veins catch fire whenever my phone buzzes with a text from her.

"Looking forward to getting this over with?" Greg asks with a grin, gesturing me toward his office, and for a second, I don't even comprehend what he means.

"Hmm?" I step inside, wait for the door to

shut.

"The reunion. Are you looking forward to all the charade stuff being done? By the way, excellent acting job, you two. You ought to get Emmys for your performances." Greg circles around to the far side of his desk and picks up a folder, passing it to me. "Here's the flight information you requested, along with schedules for the weekend—airport pickup details, hotel info, all in there. And your father's putting together a cocktail welcome night, first night we get to Greece."

I'm staring at the envelope like I've just been slapped in the face.

Greg frowns at me. "Everything all right?" His eyebrows rise. "Look, if you're worried about how this is going to go down, don't be, Jasper. She's *perfect.* Seriously. Some of those dollar store outfits she's been wearing to work lately, not to mention all the rumors all over the office? Your father is going to lose his shit when he meets her. She's his worst nightmare made manifest." Greg looks positively giddy at the thought of it. "Maybe we can start a rumor that she's planning to pawn the rock you gave her as soon as the ink's dry on the marriage license too. You know, for good measure."

I glare at him.

His expression falls, only a little. "What? I thought you guys planned all this. She's the gold-digger bride who teaches your dad a much-needed lesson about meddling in his son's affairs, when those affairs shouldn't be related to your performance at the office. No?"

"Don't talk about her like that," I say, my voice low and angry. My stomach clenches. I mean, yes, that *was* the plan. But just hearing Greg describe her like that turns my stomach.

What am I going to do if my father *does* do what we want? If he demands that I leave Dee? I went into this wanting a wife he'd hate, so he'd let me off the hook, demand I divorce her and leave me alone to take over as CEO whether I have a wife on my arm and a passel of kids underfoot or not.

But now...

Now, I'm realizing, I might not *want* to leave her. Even if Dad does demand it.

Greg, meanwhile, is staring at me like I've grown a second head. "Jasper." He crosses around to my side of the table now, and takes the files from my hands for a moment, so he can rest his hands on my shoulders and level with me, eye to eye. "Dude. I know I'm your assistant and all, but as your distant cousin... As your *friend*, are you all right? You've been acting super weird since this charade started, and now, what, you're telling me you don't want me to call her what we're currently hoping everyone here is calling her?"

"You don't understand." I brush his hands off my shoulders and reach for the file, ready to storm out.

Greg starts to laugh, then. "Oh, my God. Are you actually falling for her, Jasper?"

"Of course not," I snap, instinctively. Immediately, a surge of guilt rises in my stomach. I'm not. *Am I?*

"Did we choose too well? Did we pick the one gold-digger who's actually capable of hitting pay dirt with you? Because I don't think I've ever seen you look so riled up before, not even on the test track, let alone over some girl."

"She's not just some girl," I snap. "She's going to be my wife. At least, as far as the public knows. I won't have her talked about like this."

"So you don't want your father to hate her after all then?" Greg quirks a brow. "Because if not, she is going to need a serious makeover, and a new background story before she meets him, I gotta say —"

"I'm not listening to any more of this." I turn the doorknob, file tucked under my arm. "You're my assistant, Greg. Do as I tell you, and show my fiancée some respect." With that, I slam the door on him and head out of the building. Toward my car, where Dee will already be waiting, leaning against the hood, sunning herself the way she always does until I meet her out here to drive her home.

Home. My condo has never really felt like a home before. Not without her in it. I used to work overtime all the time, spend countless hours in the office, but now... Now I can't wait to get there. Can't wait to tear the place apart with her.

The moment Dee pushes herself off the hood of my car, smiling, arms spread wide to greet me—the moment I step into those arms and pull her body against mine, her curves melding into mine, a perfect fit, and my mouth claims hers—I feel right. I feel whole again.

Screw whatever Greg thinks. Screw what anyone thinks. She and I will figure this out together.

But as I take the wheel, and Dee picks up the sheaf of paper Greg gave me without thinking, flipping through it and exclaiming at the first class plane tickets, the fancy chain hotel name, my pulse thuds in my temples. *What if Greg included anything else?* What if he added a personal note about our initial plan or about my father's reaction?

I reach over, as casually as I can to pluck the folder from her hands. "Let's look at that later," I tell her with a sideways grin, and hope I manage to seem nonchalant as I toss the file into the backseat. Because what am I going to say if she ever finds out how all this began? If she learns that we chose her because she seemed like the least likely candidate to fit into my life, out of every single other intern in that pool?

She knows we want to fool my father into thinking I'm married, so I can be promoted to CEO. She doesn't know that the whole plan was for my father to hate her on sight, for him to disapprove so strongly that he demands I divorce her, and stops asking me to wed before I take over the company.

We chose her because she seemed like the opposite of any girl I'd ever be caught dead dating. Because we wanted her to cause the worst possible reaction among my family, because we expected everyone to whisper about her the exact same way that they're all whispering now, the gossip spreading like slow wildfire.

I couldn't bear that. Whatever happens, however all this plays out, she can't know how it began. Because it's all changed now. I see her so differently. I see this whole plan differently.

"Penny for your thoughts?" Dee asks, smiling at me as she reaches over to turn down the radio. "You look lost in them."

"Just thinking about Greece. The reunion."

She slips her hand over mine and squeezes my fingers gently. "It'll go great. Your father will see there's really chemistry between us, and I'm sure he'll buy this whole thing." The unspoken second line hovers on her lips.

And then what?

I squeeze her hand back. "You're right," I murmur. "He will. And then we'll enjoy the shit out of our Greek vacation, and my cousins will torment you, and a swarm of babies will descend upon you like locusts, until you can't wait to get out of there. I promise." I force a laugh, but when I catch her eye in the rearview mirror, she's not laughing. She's staring out the side window, gaze distant, unfocused. "That is, if you still want this to end, then," I murmur.

She brightens, a smile touching those lips once more. I notice it doesn't quite reach her eyes, though. "That's the plan, isn't it? We tell everybody we eloped right before Greece, and then after it's over, after your dad gives you the promotion you need, we... Go our separate ways."

"It was the plan," I say, careful, hesitant.

"Good," she answers, before I can say any more. Because I can add, *but it doesn't have to be.*

I let those additional words die on my lips. Turn back to the road, to my own private thoughts. If she's still on board for this, then I don't want to push her. I don't want to tangle her up in something more than she bargained for.

But… Well. I'll face this in Greece. Because at some point, before she goes, I *am* going to tell her how I feel. That's the very least I can do. The rest of this, we'll figure it out then.

****

We step into the condo, hands clasped, and Dee tosses her bag onto the couch. "So." She spins to face me, smiling once more, after our somewhat stinted, quiet car ride. "One of our last nights here, huh?"

"For now," I reply, smiling too.

"I think we'd better celebrate." She reaches for a button of the coat she's wearing. I didn't think much of the coat—it's longer than the one she normally wears, practically a trench coat, but then again, it was drizzling today.

Then she undoes the top button, and my gaze dips, interested.

I don't see anything between her collarbones but bare skin.

She keeps going, unbuttoning farther and farther, until she peels the two sides of the trench apart to reveal her toned, curvy body, completely naked beneath.

I never knew it was possible to get this fucking hard this fucking fast. "You left the office wearing that?" I lift one eyebrow, smirking.

"Changed in the bathroom before I came to meet you." She flashes me a wink, then lets the coat drop to the floor entirely. "You like?"

"I think someone's been a very naughty girl at work today." I step closer to her, and her breath hitches, her cheeks flushing in that way I love, whenever I stand too close to her, whenever her blood surges the same way mine is right now. "What are we going to do about this, hmm, little naughty girl?"

She bats her eyes, coquettish. "Whatever you think is the right punishment for such naughtiness."

"Hmm." I circle around her, drinking in the view, savoring, taking my time with her, like I always do. I trail a hand over her shoulders, down her side, just lightly enough to make her shiver at my touch.

When I've made a full circle around her, I grab a pillow from the couch and toss it at her feet. "Kneel down."

Her eyes light up, and she grins, though she also drops down onto the cushion I offer. As she does, I cross to stand in front of her, her mouth even with the straining bulge in my jeans. "Undo my jeans," I tell her. She reaches up with both hands, but I stop her with a single fingertip against her forehead. "Ah, ah. Use your mouth only."

She laughs. Then she lifts a single brow at me. "Challenge accepted."

I bite back a grin. I know my girl by now. She tackles any challenge with effort and then some. This is no different. She leans in and catches the zipper of my jeans between her teeth and eases it down. The button takes her longer, and she has to get her tongue involved, which I admit only makes the sight all the hotter. By the time she finally grips my jeans in her teeth and yanks them down to pool around my ankles, I'm so hard it's bordering on painful.

"I'm using my hands now," she tells me, with one last defiant look at me.

I laugh, but nod, and she reaches up to yank down my boxers next, as eager for me as I am for her. I suck air in through my teeth as she wraps both hands around my base and starts to stroke the length of my cock, up and down. She leans in to flick out her tongue and lap up the drop of precum that's already gathered on my tip, and just that single touch of her hot, wet tongue makes my ass clench and my whole body tense in anticipation. "You really do have a magic mouth," I tell her.

More so when she parts those sexy little Cupid's bow lips of hers and wraps them around me. I love the sight of her like this, kneeling before me, my cock stretching her lips. Her eyes find mine, and she manages to smile, even with my cock stuffed in her mouth, and I reach down to run both hands through her hair, reassuring, encouraging. "Just like that, Dee." I start to rock my hips back and forth against her, starting to take control.

Her eyelids flutter shut and she rocks with me, concentrating. At the same time, her hands delve between my legs, gently teasing my balls, a sensation that sends me spiraling higher.

"I love watching you do this," I tell her, my voice only slightly strained when she lifts her tongue and begins to run it along my length, rubbing back and forth along my underside, the tip of her tongue tracing patterns along my shaft.

I start to rock faster, getting into it now. "Seeing you on your knees like this..." I thrust into her mouth, a little deeper each time, working up to the throat-fucking I know she can handle like a goddamn champion. "Watching those tits of yours bounce."

She glances up at me then, her expression coy. She shifts a little, spreads her knees so I can see more of her body kneeling before mine, watch those breasts bounce against her chest as she stretches her jaw, expands her mouth wider, surrenders full control to me.

Sensing she's ready now, I start to thrust

harder, my tip touching the back of her throat each time, easing a little down into her throat. "Relax," I remind her when she tenses, and I dig my hands into her hair to brace myself. She listens, relaxes her jaw, and we both find our stride, as I start to fuck her mouth in earnest.

She keeps her tongue moving, stroking along me, and her lips remain clenched tight around my shaft. But it's every time my tip touches the back of her throat, slides just that little way down it, that really gets me fired up. I can't control it any longer. I fuck her faster, bracing myself with her hair, and she moans in the back of her throat, driving me wild, the vibrations echoing all throughout my body.

"I'm going to come, Dee," I hiss in a sharp breath. "Fuck, I'm going to come."

She purses those lips around me and opens wide, and when I start to come, I grab her face with both hands, pull her against me, coming deep in her throat. She swallows, grabs my ass with her hands, holding on tight as she keeps her mouth around my cock, licking and sucking until it feels like she's pulled every last drop from me.

Then she goes to work dragging that tongue along my length, cleaning me with long, steady strokes, lapping up any juices that may have escaped her earlier.

When she's finally satisfied that she's licked me clean, and leans back a little, I drop to my knees beside her and pull her against my chest, crushing her mouth with mine. Tasting my cum on her lips, feeling her lips part under mine, it's already starting to get me

excited again and we've barely finished round one.
I've never felt like this before. So hungry for
someone, so desperate to be with them, fuck them,
kiss them, pleasure them constantly. I've never known
a woman like this. We break apart, and I gaze down at
her with wonder.

"You really are a marvel, Dee."

She grins, lopsided. It's somehow cuter for
that. "Not my fault you're too addictive to quit."

"That's my line," I scold her, then lean in for
another kiss.

By the time we're supposed to be making
dinner, we've already lost track of the time and
wound up in the shower, getting not so very clean
after all. I finger her against the glass door of the
shower, her breasts pressed flat against the pane, both

of us savoring the view in the mirror on the other side as she climaxes hard, coming all over my fingers, and then when she grabs them to lick them clean, I lose my train of thought all over again.

It's like this every night. Every night we find something new to explore with one another. Every night we throw caution and all our well-laid plans to the wind—but I don't even mind, I love this so much. Being with her, pleasuring her, getting to know every little gasp and sigh. And every little corner of her mind, too, as we chat in the time between, lolling around the bed or the couch or the floor or wherever we wind up.

But later that night, after another failed attempt at cooking, another pizza delivery, and one last roll through my sheets, as I lie there in the dark, propped up on one elbow watching her drift off to sleep, her eyelids fluttering with the beginning of some dream… In that moment, after the excitement of the evening fades, all the worries of the day come creeping back in.

What if this trip goes exactly as it was supposed to go? What if my family drives a wedge between us, and she sees through my façade to exactly who I am—the kind of guy who would hire a wife in order to piss off his father. The kind of person who'd put her in an uncomfortable, awkward situation just because I thought Dad would definitely assume she's a gold-digger.

The kind of person who underestimated her. Just like everybody else is doing now.

I've learned my lesson, but what happens if

she finds out how blind I was going into this?

CHAPTER TEN

Dee

Well. This is it.

Today I leave the good old U.S. of A. for the first time in my life. I have a passport, luckily, because Mom had always dreamed about taking me overseas to Europe. She passed before that ever happened, and the passport sat in the back of my drawer, unused, unremembered. Until this job. Until this opportunity popped up.

Until I signed up for this crazy arrangement.

Now I'm rolling up to the airport with a probably way over packed suitcase—I had no idea what I'd need to wear, so I think I wound up throwing half of my closet into this bag—with a rock the size of a gumball on my left ring finger, and striding right up to the hottest guy in line for check-in.

"Hey there handsome," I greet Jasper with a smile.

He leans down to kiss me, long and slow, but there's something tense about his posture. Constrained. Like he's holding back.

"Everything okay?" I ask. I glance around surreptitiously, but I don't spy Mr. Quint Sr. anywhere in sight. Or anyone who looks like they might be related to Jasper, for that matter. I've only seen Mr. Quint from afar, and only once in the lobby of the office when I stopped in on my first day. As for the rest of the family, they're a complete mystery to me. Would I recognize his mother if I saw her? Does Jasper take after her or his father in the looks department?

But it appears to be just us on this flight, since Jasper just smiles and guides me forward in the line. "Fine. I'm just not looking forward to this jet lag, that's all."

"How rough is it going to be?" I bite my lower lip, suddenly concerned. I've never flown this far. The farthest I've flown in a plane is up to Seattle to visit some friends, and even that only a few times.

"You'll be fine." He wraps an arm around my shoulders and squeezes me once, reassuring. "I'm just being a whiner. We're in business class, after all, with fully reclining seats."

My eyes go wide. "That's a thing?"

He bursts into laughter. "Oh God. Wait until we get to the champagne and the dinner with linen and cutlery, too."

I narrow my eyes, pretending to be suspicious. "Are you rich or something, Mr. Quint?"

He snorts. "It's still the same disappointing plane food everyone else eats, I assure you, Ms. Smith. But don't worry. I've got a lounge pass, so we can stop there before we get on the plane."

Now it's my turn to laugh and roll my eyes. "So you were saying about *not* being rich?"

He grins, then turns to hand both of our passports to the airline agent. All the way through security, I trail after him, watching a series of doors open, one after the other. First they let us skip the security line, then they take us into a lounge, which is full of free alcohol, snacks that look better than half the restaurants I normally frequent, and bored-looking business types lounging around ignoring both of these things.

"You'd think all these people would want to take advantage of this delicious… Oh God is that a cheese plate?" I attack the buffet with gusto, which makes Jasper laugh and follow after to pour us both drinks.

"Is champagne really a good idea on a plane? I mean… don't you get drunker at altitude, or something?" I squint at the glasses he brings over to our table, which I have positively heaped with food.

"That just adds to the fun," he tells me with a smirk, and then he pauses to stare at the table between us. "You know we're going on a plane ride, not a weeklong safari through a jungle, right?"

"I can't help it, this is my reaction around free food. Call it an instinctual future college student behavior." I shrug one shoulder, wink, then pop a tart into my mouth. Or at least, I think it's a tart. It turns out instead to be some kind of fish paste flavored item, which makes me immediately grimace and spit it into my napkin.

Jasper watches me, torn between laughter and disgust. "The apple of my eye, ladies and gentlemen."

"I'm sure your folks will positively love me. I'll be sure to put on my best behavior at dinner—do you think there will be a buffet at the resort I can attack too?" I'm joking, but I see a flash of something in his eyes. Is that worry? I tilt my head, lean closer.

"I'm joking, Jasper."

"I'm aware. You do have a pretty obvious tell when you're being sarcastic." He tilts his head and quirks an eyebrow. "The way you always stare at me right after like you're waiting for audience laughter at the punch line."

I roll my eyes. "Well, there was no laughter forthcoming, so I figured I'd better check that you noticed the staring. Jasper, look, you've been quiet all day. Are you really not going to tell me what's bugging you? I mean… If it's about the reunion and everything… I get it. I'm a little worried too." I laugh, trying to get him to join me.

He doesn't.

"I mean, it's definitely going to be weird. But is it strange that I sort of want them to like me, even though I'm just the fake wife?" I tilt my head, try to keep things lighthearted, playful. "That's probably weird, right?"

"No," he says, his voice low and serious. Not at all playful. Not even a smile tugging at the corner of his lips. "It's not weird. I hope they like you too." But the way he says it, like that, deadpan, it makes it sound like he hopes just the opposite. Like he's being sarcastic.

My stomach flips, and I sit back in my chair, unsure of myself now. "What's Greece like?" I ask to ease the tension—mostly for myself. I don't want to think too long or hard about what it means that he's nervous right now. Or what we're about to face together.

"Beautiful. The weather's gorgeous this time

of year. And the food blows all this away." He gestures at my spread of snacks with a hint of a smile again. "You'll love it." He says it with confidence, and I believe him. I know it's only been a month now— *only a month since we agreed on this crazy plan*, somehow it feels both so much longer and like so little time has passed—but he does know me. When we go out for dinner, I never have to kick him for trying to order for us both, because he's already guessed what I want off the menu and checked with me first. And the couple times we've caught movies on TV, usually at his place after another late-night love-making session that's left us both way too awake to sleep, but way too tired to do anything but watch a screen, he always picks the cheesy rom-coms that I would've chosen.

He gets me, somehow. And I think I get him,

usually. Except like today, when he's in these wistful moods, like he's nostalgic for something that isn't even over yet.

I lean forward, elbows on my knees. "So what was our wedding like?"

His eyebrows shoot up. "Hmm?"

"We eloped, right, that's our story?" Yesterday, before we parted ways to go and pack our bags for departure this morning, he handed me a slim wedding band. He slid a matching titanium one on his own ring finger, which I have to admit, I stole admiring peeks as he did. There's something hot about seeing it on him; that thin little reminder that, for now at least, he's mine and mine alone.

My husband, in name if not deed.

"It is." He's nodding.

"So, I think we need a story. Justice of the peace, or…?"

"Mm." He scratches his chin. "Does that make a good enough story for the grandkids, though?"

I laugh. "Okay, how about this. We hired one of those online minister people—"

"Those *what?*"

"Do you live in the real world or just your rich bubble?" I elbow him and roll my eyes.

"Little from column A, little from column B…" he replies.

"Okay, people can get certificates to perform weddings online. You can hire them for cheap. Let's say we got one of them—"

"So not Vegas?" he cuts in.

I snort. "You think the justice of the peace isn't a good enough tale for the grandkids, but *Vegas* is? How cliché is that?"

"We could've gone somewhere fun in Vegas. Maybe one of those drive-through chapels."

I roll my eyes. "I like my idea better. Online minister guy marries us on the beach."

"Why the beach?" He tilts his head, genuinely curious, it seems.

"Because it's romantic as hell, duh. And because if you dip your toes in the surf while you're doing it, it's like getting married between worlds, halfway between the land and the sea…" I drift off, staring into space a little, and he smirks at me.

"Someone's a closet romantic."

"When did you figure that out, sometime

around our third re-watch of *Ten Things I Hate About You?*"

"I'm only watching it for Heath Ledger, dunno about you."

I laugh and elbow him again, and we dissolve into easy banter. For a while, it's easy to forget what this trip means. Where we're headed. All the unanswered questions waiting on the other side. But then it's time to board our plane, and the worry comes rushing right back as we walk through the priority boarding lane (of course) and into our crazy nice seats. He's right—they really do recline all the way back. I didn't even know seats on airplanes had that option!

I am definitely going to be ruined for budget airlines after this trip. But for now, I take advantage of the luxury and bundle myself into one of the blankets (is it just me or are these nicer in first class too? Fuzzier somehow?) and curl up beside Jasper, reaching out to catch his hand as we prepare for takeoff. His wedding ring digs into my finger, the band cool and solid, and I stroke it without thinking, unconscious.

Jut then, a small toy crashes down in the aisle next to me, and I hear a wail start up. I glance over to find a toddler in the seat a row over, kicking his little chubby legs and pointing at the toy he's dropped, a little red sports car. I flash him a reassuring smile and lean down to grab it for him, quickly handing it over to stave off any farther freak-outs.

"You know, my husband and I build cars like this one," I tell him as I pass it back to him, trying that word on for size. *Husband.*

His mother smiles at me gratefully, and the little boy accepts the toy with huge eyes, too busy staring at me now to remember the car. "Really?" he asks. "That's a job you can do?"

"Of course. But the cars we make are people-sized." I wink at him. "Even more fun."

He spins to his mother, eyes still huge. "Mommy, I want to do that when I grow up!"

When I settle back into my seat and reach for Jasper's hand again, I notice that for the first time since we got onto this flight, he's actually smiling. "What?" I ask, accusatory.

He just laughs. "Nothing, nothing." He squeezes my hand, tight enough that the wedding band presses against my skin. "Just... You said husband."

"Figured we'd better start practicing now, no?" I lift a brow.

He, in turn, raises my hand to his lips. He kisses my fingers, one after the other, eyes locked on mine. "I don't think I'll need a reminder," he says. "I rather like calling you wife."

My stomach does a happy flip then, and not just because we've taxied to the end of the runway and finally begun takeoff.

CHAPTER ELEVEN

Jasper

Showtime, I think as the prearranged car Dad sent for us pulls up in front of the resort. Between all of our family members, we've practically booked up this entire island, let alone this whole resort. But my gaze darts right to my father first and foremost, standing front and center with an arm around my mother's shoulders, watching our car pull in.

He arrived on an earlier flight. I took this later one on purpose, to delay as long as possible the moment when he and Dee meet. I've been enjoying having her all to myself, this secret partner-in-crime.

Now, it's all about to come to a head. And this girl who I picked especially to piss him off, to make him think she won't fit in...

She's turning into the one I want him to like best. That moment on the plane, hearing her call me her husband so casually while she passed that little boy his toy, laughing and talking with him... That made it hit home. I want that with her. I want a family with her. I want *her*.

"You ready for this?" Dee squeezes my fingertips, pulling me back to the present, like she can sense what I'm thinking.

She's always able to do that. I cast her a tiny sideways smile. "Ready as I'll ever be. But what about you? You're the one about to face the firing squad."

She bursts into laughter. "You keep saying

family is everything, and then you talk about them like they're the scariest thing on the planet."

"Who says they can't be both?" I flash her a wry smile, and then the valet is there, opening our car doors, and we climb out to face the music. "Dad," I call over the top of the car, hoping to catch his attention first.

But his eyes have locked onto Dee already. I watch him and Mom do a once-over. She's dressed in sweatpants and an oversized hoodie, but then, we did just fly 10 hours to get here. Surely they can't blame her for that.

"Mom, Dad." I smoothly step between them for the introductions. "I'd like to introduce Dee. My wife."

My mother's eyes widen, and she shoots my

father a sideways glare that nobody for a mile around could miss. "I thought you were joking, Antoine."

"I wouldn't joke about something like this," my father replies, his poker face on-point as he smiles and extends a hand to Dee. "It's so lovely to meet you."

"Great to meet you too!" She goes for the hug before she notices his extended hand instead, and drops her arms, face flushed, to shake his hand. "And you too, Mrs. Quint." She offers a hand to my mother, who stares between Dee, me and my father like she's utterly bewildered by this turn of events.

I wonder how much my father told her. If he shared his little stipulation with her about promoting me to CEO. If she knows he's responsible for the sudden wife appearance.

"Please, call me Kara." Finally, she takes Dee's hand and squeezes her fingers, just once, in the signature weird handshake my mother always does to throw businessmen off. They never know quite what to do when she doesn't try to pump their arm off shaking hands. "It's a pleasure to meet you, although I do wish my son had introduced you sooner." She flashes me a pointed glare. "Perhaps we could have properly celebrated your nuptials as a family, rather than hearing about it second-hand through a secretary."

My ears go red. "Mom, I—"

"It was my idea, Mrs. Quint," Dee interrupts, blurting out the words. Then she winces in apology. "I mean, Kara. I just... I don't have any family left, and I'd always loved the idea of eloping. It's so

291

romantic, don't you think? We went to the beach for it, and had one of those ministers from… um… online…" Her practiced recital of our wedding story dies on her lips at my mother's cool, silent stare.

Her lack of words says far more than anything Mom could say.

"That sounds lovely," Dad butts in, and none of us miss the subtle way he taps Mom's shoulder with his fingertips.

"Yes, quite lovely. I'm so sorry that we couldn't be there for it," Mom replies. "But I'm glad you both enjoyed it."

"How did you meet?" Dad asks, cutting straight past the wedding topic. Damn. I should have guessed this would hurt Mom's feelings, not being invited to her only son's elopement. What a tangled mess we've made here. Maybe she'll forgive me someday, when I explain what all this was really about.

"Oh, uh…" I cast Dee a glance.

She bursts into laughter. "Well, it was pretty damn strange, actually, I was…"

Mom's eyebrows shoot higher at the word *damn*, and Dee flushes all over again.

"She's one of our interns," interrupts another voice. All four of us turn to find Greg at our elbows, having finished putting the poor resort staff through their paces organizing my relatives' rooms and bags. "Jasper was taken with her on the first day, when she came to introduce herself at the water cooler." He flashes me a reassuring, *I've got this* smile.

I want to kick him. I know he thinks he's helping, reinforcing the whole look-at-this-random-intern-your-son-just-married story, but this is *not* the direction I want to go with anymore. "Dee's great, actually," I interrupt. "It was funny, the first day we met, before her orientation, I took her out on the test track…" I flash Dad a glance. "You should see how she handles the cars out there. And not just on the road, she knows her way around beneath a hood, too."

"I see." Mom blinks at me slowly, and only then do I hear the way those words sound. *Beneath a hood.*

"So you're into cars?" Dad perks up, zeroing in on a common subject of interest to chat about.

"Oh yeah, it's what drew me to the company in the first place. I've always been a fan." Dee beams at him, and launches into her story about growing up ogling Quint cars on the road, daydreaming about one day being able to work at designing something that beautiful and functional all in one. By the time she's waxing poetic about her spin around the test track, I can tell that Dad, at least, is into the conversation.

Mom, on the other hand, shoots me a concerned glance and gently disentangles herself from my father's grasp. "Jasper, can we speak for a moment?" she asks, her voice low.

"Of course, Mom."

I step off to the side, somewhat worried about leaving Dee and Dad alone with Greg. Greg flashes me another thumbs-up, and my worry only increases.

But there's nothing I can do about it with Mom breathing down my neck right now. "I hope you got a pre-nup," Mom says, straight off.

My face goes red. "*Mother.*"

"Well, honestly, Jasper. Who is this girl? How long have you known her?"

"A month."

"One month, and you're ready to run off and marry her without so much as mentioning her to any of the family first?" She purses her lips.

"I told Dad about it. He seemed supportive."

"Your father wants grandchildren so badly he'd support you eloping with a complete stranger. Which, you've practically done, I might add. So, like father like son." Mom groans and waves a hand back over her shoulder toward her husband.

"How long did you and Dad know each other before you got married?" I counter.

"That was a different time," she replies.

But I already know the answer. "He proposed to you on your third date," I remind her. "You got married at a secret ceremony with the justice of the peace because your dad didn't approve. How long after your third date was that?"

"Six months, not one," she replies, one eyebrow arched wryly. "And as I said, it was a different time. Besides, our families had known one another for years before that. My father and Antoine's may not exactly have been friends, but they were aware of one another, ran in the same social circles."

"So you don't approve because she's not rich, is that it?" I roll my eyes.

"I'm saying that when you are a member of a family like the Quints, when you have the kind of

297

resources we do, Jasper, people will try to take advantage of that. *Women* will try to take advantage of that."

"What, you don't think any gay male gold-diggers out there would try to seduce me too?" I press a hand to my chest, feigning shock.

Mom's mouth tightens around the edges. "This is not a joke, Jasper. This is about your inheritance, your family, your livelihood. If this girl is some, some… snake in the grass—"

"Give her a chance, Mom. Get to know her before you judge her." I arch a brow. "And if it makes you feel any better, she has no legal grounds to take me for all the money I'm worth, okay?" I don't say pre-nup, because there wasn't even a wedding. But if implying there's some sort of legal protection in place will reassure Mom, then I'll run with it.

At that, Mom sighs, and her shoulders relax a little. "All right. I'm sorry, Jasper. I just…" It's only then that I notice the tears stinging the corners of her eyes. "I thought you'd invite your father and me to your wedding, that's all."

Shit. This is the real reason she's upset. Not the gold-digging stuff—although I'm sure that's a concern, it's not what has her so emotional. "Oh, Mom…" I reach out my arms. Wrap them around her, and peer over her head at Dad and Dee in the distance, both chatting with Greg now.

Dee, for her part, has shrunken back in on herself, pulled her hands into the sleeves of her oversized hoodie while they talk. Dad looks, if anything, more worried than Mom by now.

299

What is Greg saying over there?

Crap. "I'm sorry, Mom," I tell her, and lean down to kiss her cheek. "I'll make it up to you, I promise. It was a spur-of-the-moment thing. We'll do a real ceremony at some point, I'm sure."

She draws in a deep, shaky breath. "Okay. I'm sorry I overreacted. I know you've never fallen so quickly before, Jasper, so I'm sure this Dee must really be something to have won you over." Then Mom follows my gaze over her shoulder, and spies her husband's face. "Oh dear. But we'd better go and save her from your father."

We part and cross back over to Dad's side.

"—sounds like it's been very difficult," Dad is saying.

Dee shuffles her feet, clearly uncomfortable.

"I mean… Some things about it."

"I don't know how you put up with it," Greg put in. "I'd feel awful, if I knew people all throughout the office were spreading those kinds of stories about me."

"What's this?" I break in, voice sharp. "Are we really talking office politics here?" I gesture around us at the blue skies overhead, the bright Mediterranean sun beating down on the beautiful cliff side resort that overlooks blue waves and white sand beaches far below. Beaches I can't wait to bring Dee to—and not just because it will be a great excuse to see her in a bikini. Or even just bikini bottoms—a lot of the beaches here are topless ones. I bet she'd fit right in, with that sexy, curvy body of hers…

Then again, do I want all the other Greek

men on the beach ogling my wife? I'm torn.

"Sorry, Jasper." Greg tilts his head at me, his expression confused and conflicted. I'll need to talk to him later. Explain that this whole lambast-Dee thing is no longer the plan. The new plan is to make her feel as comfortable as possible amidst my crazy family.

"I think Dee and I need to go drop our things off," I say, with a glance past my family at the hotel attendants. Our bags have already been moved up to the room, and one attendant is waiting discretely nearby with a pair of key cards. "Freshen up a bit. What's the plan for tonight again?"

"Cocktails on the rooftop lounge deck at sunset," Greg pipes up helpfully, clearly trying to make up for my annoyance at him.

"Great. See you all there." I lean in to kiss Mom's cheek goodbye, then hug Dad. They both embrace Dee this time, at least, rather than offering handshakes. But I notice Dad's hug seems stiff and formal, and Mom's still tense, despite her promise to me to give Dee a real chance.

By the time we make it to our room, Dee's shoulders sag and she lets out a huge sigh. "Well that couldn't have gone worse," she groans.

"They're going to love you," I insist, shutting the door behind us and crossing the room to open the huge balcony windows. They overlook the sea, and the view is breathtaking, with little dots of green islands in the distance and the beautiful red-tiled rooftops of the village down below us. "Just give them some time to get to know you, that's all. They're in shock."

She runs a hand through her hair, not even the view or the delicious-smelling sea breeze distracting her right now. "I guess it doesn't really matter, at the end of the day, right?" She offers up a wry smile. "It's probably stupid, but part of me… Part of me wanted them to like me anyway. I don't know." She shrugs one shoulder, lets it fall.

I cross to the bed and sit beside her, then wrap an arm around her shoulders to tug her against me. "They will, Dee, believe me. I know my parents. Mom is hurt about the elopement, which, to be honest, I should have seen coming. But her and Dad's romance wasn't so difference—they moved crazy fast when they got married, even for their generation. And Dad… he's going to be over the moon by dinnertime.

This is what he always wanted for me, after all," I add with a wry smile.

"A wife, yeah. But probably not a wife like me." It's killing me to see her shoulders slumped like this. "And what was with Greg? I thought he liked me, but today…"

I scowl. "I'm going to talk to him." *He thinks he's doing me a favor,* is what I don't—can't—say. After the cocktail party tonight, I'm just going to have to catch him alone and explain that the plan has changed. Things aren't what they used to be. This whole situation is quicksand under my feet.

In the meantime, I nudge Dee with my shoulder. "Come on. Let's get ready. If you're going to wow my parents, might as well start with this party tonight."

"Step one: I need to stop swearing, don't I? Your mom about turned white when I said *damn*." She laughs and pushes herself off the bed, then offers me a hand. I take it and pull her back down onto my lap instead, kissing her hard.

"Mm, please don't stop. I love your dirty mouth." I trace my tongue along her lower lip, and she parts it for me, draws my lower lip between her teeth to bite down gently.

"You do, huh?" When we break apart, her eyes are full of mischief.

"Especially when you're using said dirty mouth to tell me all the dirty things you want me to do to you," I reply with an arched brow, as I flip her around beneath me. With the sea breeze fluttering the curtains, and our view out over one of the most beautiful cities this side of the Atlantic—and most importantly, with Dee pinned underneath me, her body wriggling in anticipation as she wraps her arms around my neck and pulls me down against her— today should be perfect. This whole week should be.

It will be. I'll make it right. For both of us.

CHAPTER TWELVE

Dee

Jasper and I, predictably, take a bit longer to prep for the cocktail party than we anticipated. As in a couple of hours longer. Finally, I manage to shower without him dragging me back into the stream of water, and get dressed in the only cocktail-hour type dress I brought. I got it at a vintage shop, knee-length and lacy, and it reminds me of a ballerina's costume, but with a little edge from the studs sewn into the top and the ragged fringe on the hem.

I check myself out in the mirror before departing our suite, and I actually smile. I like the look on me.

But the moment Jasper and I step arm-in-arm through the veranda onto the rooftop bar of the resort, my stomach sinks. I've gone all wrong with this. His cousins—these must be the cousins, there are about a thousand of them, and everyone has the same dark messy waves as Jasper, the same piercing dark eyes—are in veritable ball gowns, all sleek black things, some clingy and others flowy. But nothing like my dress. Nothing that looks so casual or… well, *cheap*, in comparison.

My cheeks flush immediately. But then a woman rushes forward to grasp my hand and pull me into a hug, without so much as an introduction first.

"You must be Dee," she says, all in one breath. "I'm Sofia, Jasper's cousin. It's so lovely to meet you—and so *wonderful* our little J's gotten himself a girl at last, huh?" She winks at him. Only then do I notice the train of boys clinging to the hem of Sofia's gown. Each one dressed cuter than the last, in little matching suits. "Oh, these are my sons. Peter, Christopher, Luke. The girls are floating around here somewhere too…"

"Two," pipes up one of the boys.

Sofia laughs. "Luke Two," she amends. "Luke number one is his uncle. At least whenever we're at big family events like this." Then she glances at me with a grin. "I tried to explain the proper term is junior, but—"

"I'm not junior," the boy—Luke Two, I suppose—replies, looking cross.

"Of course you're not." Jasper kneels and

extends his arms. "Hey there, Two. How you been?"

"Good." Luke Two considers Jasper for a moment, then, with a laugh and a huge smile, peels away from his mother's skirts and his brothers to throw his arms around Jasper's neck in a hug. The other two boys join in, and pretty soon Jasper is rolling on the ground of the very fancy, very elite rooftop club with these kids.

I can't help it—I burst into laughter, loving the sight. Loving that he's the type of person willing to get down and dirty with his cousins' kids, even at a fancy event like this.

Sofia tucks her arm through mine as the boys continue to wrestle. "Come on," she whispers conspiratorially in my ear. "While he's distracted, let me steal you away."

She leads me straight toward the buffet table, and I think I love her already.

Along the way, we collect a couple of other cousins—Chloe and Jessie, who come to offer Sofia congratulations, both with significant glances at her stomach.

"Are you pregnant?" I ask, genuinely surprised, because I couldn't tell under her tight, form-fitting gown.

"Four months along, bless you." She pats my hand and laughs. "I love this girl," she adds to Chloe, who falls in beside us at the buffet. "Great taste in food and compliments."

The three of us stock up our plates and hover at the edge of the party chatting. Sofia points out Jasper's aunts and uncles and various cousins. I lose track of most people—there are so many names flying past, it's hard to attach them all to faces. But Sofia just pats my arm, reassuring. "Don't worry, you'll get to know them all soon enough. In the meantime, just stick with me, and I'll make sure to whisper hints anytime your memory needs a jog."

"Thank you," I tell her, sincerely. "It is a little overwhelming, but in a good way—it must be so wonderful to have a huge family like this."

"Wonderful and the bane of my existence all at once," she says with a loving sigh that makes her sound just like Jasper. "I love them to pieces, but sometimes we can be a bit much to handle. Especially for newcomers who aren't used to it. Do you have a big family, Dee?" She smiles at me, so genuine I can't help but return it.

"No, unfortunately. Just me."

"Not anymore," she corrects me with a wink. "You've got us now."

My heart soars even as my stomach sinks. Because I don't, not really. This is all for show, and sooner or later, Jasper's going to have to break the news to these people. I'm nothing more than a business agreement, a fake wife he needed to get his CEO promotion. What will his parents think of me then? They'll probably hate me even more than when they thought I was just some gold-digger.

"Oh, come here, you have to meet my brother Alex—Alex!" She shouts and waves at a guy in the crowd, who's got an infant tucked under one arm and one of the most beautiful women I've ever seen wrapped around the other.

314

I force a smile back onto my face and try to push those thoughts to the back of my mind. I try to forget that I'm faking, that none of these people are really my family now. I try to forget Jasper and I are lying to everyone here. Instead, I just focus on the party, the fun. The sense of welcome and ease which was missing when I first stepped out of the cab jet-lagged and tired earlier, but which is starting to return with every spin around the room.

Maybe... maybe I really could fit in here, I start to think.

****

Pleasantly buzzed from the cocktail Sofia pressed on me to drink in her stead—something

315

called ouzo, which tastes like licorice, but when mixed with a full glass of ice water, was actually surprisingly refreshing... And potentially deadly. I drained the whole thing before Sofia realized and stopped me, laughing, with a warning about the high alcohol content.

It definitely didn't *taste* that strong going down. It tasted delicious and light.

Now, however, as my head swims and I stumble along the hall trying to remember which suite Jasper and I are in, the floor swaying under my feet, I realize she was right. *Whoops.*

I squint at the doors and try to force the numbers to align themselves properly in my head. 403? No... 401? I sway back and forth between the two, then finally grip the knob of 403 just as it turns under my hand. "Oh—sorry!" I blurt, only to find myself face-to-face with Greg.

He hesitates, eyebrows lifted, and then smiles with understanding. "Oh. You two are next door, Dee."

"Thanks." I sway on the spot a little, but don't make a move to reach for 401. Instead, I'm too busy staring up at Greg. Greg, who I thought was my friend. Greg, who hired me for this gig in the first place, and then tried to throw me under the bus the second I got here. "Can I ask you something?" I say. I'm proud that only the *s* comes out a little slurry.

"Of course." He blinks, taken aback. Like he has no idea what he did.

"Why did you say all that stuff about me to Jasper's dad? That I was an intern who threw myself

317

at him, that people are gossiping about me…"

He tilts his head, confused. "Well, it's all true, isn't it? I mean, minus the throwing yourself at him part, but that was the party line we'd agreed to go with, I thought."

"It's just the *way* you said it, though. It made… it makes this all sound so much worse than it is."

"Worse than faking a marriage with someone your father will hate so he'll promote you to CEO and beg you to divorce her on top of that?" Greg laughs. "Yes, I suppose that does sound pretty bad, Dee, but you knew what you were signing up for."

I reel back from him, until my back hits the far wall. I glance up and down the hallway, worried someone else overheard that, my head buzzing.

"What did you just say?"

Greg frowns. Crosses the hallway to lift my chin and peer down at me. "Dee. You know this is all fake right?" His voice drops low, concerned now.

I shake my head, twist out of his grip. "Not that. The other thing. Someone your father will hate?" My chest hurts. My stomach, too. I feel like I'm going to be sick, and not just from the alcohol.

His frown deepens. "I thought you knew that's why we picked you."

We? My heart aches. "Why?" I whisper, through cracked lips.

"Jasper's father was demanding he marry in order to promote him. Jasper figured this would kill two birds with one stone. He marries for the promotion, but somebody totally inappropriate, someone his parents would think was a gold-digger just using Jasper for his money, somebody uncultured, so they'd be fine when he goes to—or, even encourage him to—divorce you."

So that's why. All Jasper's talk about liking me for me, about how I wooed him with my love of cars, about how he couldn't resist me… And all along this has been his plan. Seduce me because I'm the most humiliating option. The one who will never fit in, the one who doesn't match his family at all.

"Is it really that surprising?" Greg asks, still with that sympathetic look on his face, which somehow makes it so much worse. "I mean, you met his parents, you saw their reactions even before I said anything. You were at the party tonight, too—didn't you notice how you stood out like a sore thumb?"

The backs of my eyes sting. *I have to get out of here.* "I... I didn't really..."

"Oh, Dee." Greg reaches up to touch my shoulder, the sympathy melting into abject pity now. "I'm so sorry. I didn't think ahead about what this would feel like for you. I thought you'd be prepared for it, but how could you be? I mean, dozens of people all disapproving of you, and those girls at the office spreading all those rumors... It must have been awful."

It should have been, I think. But instead... Right up until this minute, right up until I learned what Jasper really thinks about me... Until now it hasn't been awful. It's felt like it's worth it. All this pain, all the rumors and the gossip. It was worth it to be with him, to feel like I'd finally found a guy who gets it.

Who gets *me*.

But he doesn't. Not really. I've just been a ploy all along. Somebody to toy with and then throw aside. A tool to help accomplish his goals.

Tears spill over the edge of my eyes and track down my cheeks. "Yeah, I… It has been," I whisper.

"Come here." Greg pulls me into a hug, which surprises me, but I let him, sighing. "You don't have to stay," he says. "The main part's been done. They've all seen you exist, they know who you are. If you want to go now, I don't blame you. Hell, it could even play better that way—we can say something like, you didn't like anyone here and decided to head home, and that will just make Jasper's dad even more likely to regret forcing his son into this. And then you don't have to stick around here feeling miserable all week.

How does that sound?"

For all that he hurt me with what he said earlier, Greg is making a lot of sense. I bite the inside of my cheek and nod at him. Whether this messes up Jasper's plan or not, I can't stay here any longer. Not knowing what I know now. Not feeling how I do. I need to get out of here.

I need to go home.

CHAPTER THIRTEEN

Dee

Tears sting at my eyes as I grab my suitcase and stuff it full of clothes. I hear a knock at the door, and start to cross toward it, expecting Greg. He went to pull the car around and come pick me up.

But instead I hear Jasper on the far side. "Dee? Where'd you go?" His voice sounds nearly as slurry as mine—probably from the ouzo his cousins have been forcing on everybody in sight.

I cross over to the door and pull it open, without taking the chain off the lock, so it only opens a couple of inches.

The moment he sees my face, my eyes red and swollen from crying, his eyes go wide. "What's wrong?" he blurts.

"Did you ask me to marry you because you knew your parents would hate me?" I demand.

He blinks a few times, clearly trying to clear his head. And failing. "Did I..."

"Did you choose me because I'm the most humiliating option?" My voice rises an octave now. I can't help it. It cracks on the end, and another tear spills down my cheek. I wipe it away, trying to channel anger instead of pain.

"Dee, let me in and we can talk about this..."

"Why should I? You lied to me."

"I didn't lie—"

"You said you just wanted a fake wife. Not a

fake gold-digger. Is that really what you think of me? You agree with all those angry girls at work, is that it?"

"No. Dee, listen to me, that's not how I feel anymore."

"But it was." My eyes glitter now, the tears hanging suspended, unshed.

"Please, Dee. Let me explain."

"You had weeks to explain, Jasper. You could have told me what the real plan was when we first met. Or any moment since. All this time, I thought…" A hiccup escapes my lips, frustrating me. "I thought things were changing between us. But I guess only for me."

"No, they've changed for me too. Let me in, Dee, so we can talk about this."

But I'm already pulling the ring off my finger and shoving it back at him through the crack in the door. "I'm done playing charades, Jasper. I'm done trying to fit in somewhere that I don't. And right now, we're both drunk, and in no state to talk about things, so please just…" I close my eyes. The tears spill over. "Please just go, okay? Please."

He hesitates. Hovers before the door still. "Dee…"

"*Please go*, Jasper."

"Okay," he finally whispers, after a long moment. "But only because you asked me to. And only because you're right, we should talk about this not…" He waves a hand in the air. "Not drunk."

I wait until he's gone. Until his stumbling footsteps fade down the hallway outside, until the hotel around me falls quiet.

Then I go back to the suitcase I have open on the bed, and continue to toss my things inside it. Ready to go the moment that... *Ah*. There it is. My phone buzzes with a single ring. The signal from Greg. I tap the screen and find a text from him. *Downstairs waiting*. Then I grab my suitcase, zip it shut, and I slip out of the resort.

I can't wait around anymore. I can't sit here and listen to more lies, surrounded by a family of people who despise me. Maybe when I get home, Jasper and I can talk about this on familiar territory, if he really wants to explain why he lied to me and hired me to be a gold-digger. But right now...

I'm going home.

CHAPTER FOURTEEN

Jasper

I stumble back upstairs to the party. The music is still playing, my cousins are still drinking and laughing, and the kids have gone to bed, so now the adults have really let loose. While I normally enjoy myself chatting to my cousins, especially Sofia and Chloe, tonight I can't relax. I can't think about anything but Dee, downstairs in our hotel room, her eyes red-rimmed from crying.

Crying because I didn't tell her the truth. I didn't tell her the whole story, which I should've done a long time ago. But I thought she'd react... well, like this, when I did. And I didn't want to lose her.

The irony of that hits home like a bolt. I didn't want to lose her, so I wasn't completely honest, and now I'm probably going to lose her.

Someone slaps me on the back. I grimace and turn around to excuse myself, but then I freeze. Because I've just found myself face-to-face with my father.

"Dad."

"Jasper." He's smiling, so that's something. He also has the biggest glass of ouzo I've ever seen him drink in one hand, so that could be the only reason why.

I tense. The last thing I need right now is a fight, much less a fight over the propriety of the girl I've chosen. The girl he *forced* me into choosing.

The girl I'm about to lose, who just might be the best thing in my life.

"If you're here to tell me to break things off with her, you don't need to bother," I say.

To my surprise, Dad's brow crunches up in distress. "Why on earth would I tell you to do that, son? She's your wife."

She's not. But at this point, she feels like it. She calls me husband. She's wearing my ring—or, well... she *was*. I feel its weight now, heavy in my pocket, and it only makes my heart ache worse. "I thought you'd hate her," I reply, my tone glum.

But Dad just laughs, deep and loud. "Son." He claps me on the back again, and shakes my shoulder a little. He's definitely had one too many of those ouzos. "Why would it matter what I think of her? What matters to me is that she makes you happy, Jasper. That's all I've ever wanted for you. The same happiness your mother and I found together. The same happiness we found doubly strong when we had you. So, are you happy when you're with her?"

I grit my teeth together. It's hard to think about this right now, given the mess everything has become. But when I clear my mind and think back to all the times we shared ... when I think about our first weekend away together—and not just about our hot our chemistry in the bedroom, but the times we had exploring the boardwalk and the shops, or the times driving around aimlessly, just enjoying the feeling of being on the road... Or the long talks we had late into the night, side-by-side curled up in bed.

I think about how much we have in common.

How I light up every time she enters a room, even if she's just walking past on the far side of the office, and I catch a glimpse of her on my way into a meeting.

I open my mouth, but Dad shakes his head.

"You don't even have to say it, son," he tells me. "It's written all over your face. You love her."

Love. It sinks in, deep.

I've never really been in love. I teased Dee about that, teased her for never having felt like she was in love before. But neither had I, really. I wasn't even sure I was now, until I hear Dad say the words. *I love her.* I love Dee. I really do.

"I do, Dad," I murmur.

"There you go, then." He slaps my back once more, chuckling. "As for what I think of her, Jasper, not that my opinion matters, but—I think she's refreshing. A much needed down-to-earth presence in this family. And your mother will recover from the shock—it's really just the suddenness of all this that got to her, not the wedding or Dee herself."

"Yeah, well, who's to blame for that?" I point out with a halfhearted glare at him. I'm smiling underneath it, though. Still reeling from the realization of how I feel about Dee. *Love.*

"I apologize for pushing you so hard about getting a wife," Dad says. But he's smiling beneath that apology, too. "But it worked out, didn't it? You're happy now? So, really, I think in the long run, you ought to be thanking me..."

I elbow him. "Don't get carried away, Dad. And I think you've had plenty of this to drink by now." I pluck the ouzo from his hands.

He rolls his eyes. "Fine, I'll soldier on without any thanks for all of my hard work in convincing my eternal bachelor of a son to finally settle down. But you know what I'm going to start in on next, don't you?" He lifts his eyebrows significantly.

"Don't even start," I groan.

"I would make an excellent grandfather, you know."

"Dad."

"I'm just saying." He smiles, and his gaze drifts away from me. Finds my mother instead. "You understand it now, though, don't you? The desire to start a family, once you've found the perfect person to begin one with?"

My heart begins to pound, deep in my chest. I

think about Dee's smile. Her laughter. How perfect that smile and that laugh would sound coming from an adorable little baby like the one my cousin Alexander is toting around right now. Or on a toddler like one of Sofia's little devils.

I think about Dee carrying my child, wearing my wedding ring on her finger for real, not a fake one, and my heart swells so hard it could burst. "I get it, Dad," I admit, my voice low. "I really do get it, now."

CHAPTER FIFTEEN

Jasper

Late that night, well past midnight, after the whole clan has finally stumbled to bed, I make my way back to our suite. I know she's probably still pissed. I told my cousin Alexander the bare details, and secured a place on his couch for the night, in case this chat doesn't go the way that I hope.

But Dee was drunk earlier, and so was I, and she'd just learned what a jerk I was when she and I first met. Besides, I have some things to tell her. Important things about how I really feel. So I'm hopeful that this attempt at a conversation will go more smoothly than the last.

But when I reach our suite and try the doorknob, it's open. And when I push the door open, I find our room empty, the windows still open from where I unlatched the balcony window earlier, the curtains fluttering in the breeze. My heart seizes in my chest, a premonition hitting me. On instinct, I cross to the far side of the room, to where we stowed our suitcases.

Only my slim black leather bag is there. Not the hot pink wheeled and overstuffed bag Dee packed.

My stomach churns.

I turn and race out of the room, heart pounding. I scan the hallway, but of course, she's not there. I race down to the lobby, taking the steps two at a time.

Halfway across the lobby, I run headlong into Greg, dressed in a coat and carrying car keys, which he drops into his pocket. "Hey, man, where's the fire?" He half-grins at me. The smile falls away at once, though, when he catches a real look at my expression.

"Where's Dee?" I cry out.

His eyebrows shoot skyward. "Dee?"

"Yes, you know, Dee, the girl I came here with, *my wife*, where is she?"

"Whoa, man, calm down." Greg reaches out to grip my shoulders. "Hey, come here, let's talk somewhere a little less..." He glances around the lobby. I realize, belatedly, there are a couple of other late-night stragglers here, other hotel guests, ones I

339

don't recognize. Some of the few unlucky souls stuck sharing this resort with our whole brood.

"Okay." I trail after him into a side room, a little waiting room area for hotel guests. When we're alone, though, I explode again. "Her suitcase is gone. Our room is empty. I need to find her; she's never even been out of the country before, and she doesn't speak Greek, she won't know where she's going—"

"Calm, calm. Deep breaths." Greg coaxes me, and waves for my attention. "I know where she is, Jasper."

My eyes light up. "You do? She's safe? Take me there right now."

"Not until you get control of yourself, dude. What the hell is this all about? First she's freaking out, now it's you, God, the two of you are almost as messy as real newlyweds."

"She was freaking out because she learned that you and I pinpointed her for a gold-digger lookalike, and that's why I decided to fake marry her," I say.

"Yeah, well, I'm sorry for letting that one slip, but I sort of figured you'd told her the whole plan already. You two seemed pretty chummy, so I thought you would've let her in on all the details…"

"Well, I didn't, okay?" I rake my hands through my hair. "I didn't because I didn't want her to know *why* we picked her. I didn't want to hurt her feelings. I thought… I thought she'd do this." I fling my arms wide. "And now she's run off in a foreign country—where did she go, anyway?"

"The airport."

341

My stomach hits the floor. No, it passes through it, down into the wine cellar. "What?"

"She wanted to go home. She was really upset about how your parents reacted to her, and I think the stress of so many people spreading rumors about her at work was getting to her too, so I thought I'd help by…" He breaks off, because I've grabbed the lapels of his jacket and started to shake him.

"What flight, Greg? Dammit, just…" I shove him off. "Get the car. Drive me to the airport."

"Jasper, it's taking off in…" He pauses to check his watch. "Five minutes. It's past midnight. Let's just go to bed, and in the morning you can call her and apologize—"

"That's not good enough," I snap.

"What has gotten into you? I thought this was

342

what you wanted!" Greg flings his arms wide. "You wanted a wife who'd piss off your family, well, storming off in the middle of the big reunion is just about the best possible way to do that, no?"

"I love her," I blurt.

Greg freezes where he's standing, arms still flung wide. He stares at me like a cartoon caricature of himself, shocked into silence for once.

"I love her," I repeat, louder now. "And I want her to be my actual wife. Not my fucking fake one. So if you want to keep your cushy assistant's job, drive me to the airport right now, because I'm way too drunk to get behind a wheel still, but…"

"Say no more." Greg has already spun on his heel and begun dashing toward the parking lot. I race after him, hard on his heels. "Try calling her," he shouts over his shoulder. "Tell her not to get on the flight."

Oh. Duh. Drunk me is an idiot. As I race after Greg, I fish in my pocket for my cell phone. We climb into the car, and I hit Dee's number. Wait for the ringtone.

Predictably, it goes to voicemail on the second ring. She's screening my calls. Which, after all this, I can't exactly say that I blame her for.

I try a text instead, which will be less easy to ignore.

DO NOT BOARD FLIGHT PLEASE.

WAIT FOR ME.

I HAVE TO TALK TO YOU.

The all caps also might be overkill, but I'm hoping it will get my currently very desperate and somewhat drunken point across. Greg, meanwhile, true to his word, floors the accelerator and speeds us along the narrow, twisting highways toward the airport. It was about a half an hour drive, if I remember correctly from when we landed here what feels like a lifetime ago. Was that really only this morning?

My head swims.

My pulse pounds.

We make it to the airport in 20 minutes. Greg takes after most of the employees at our company when it comes to driving. We'll probably be mailed a speeding ticket—they're better about speed cameras here in Greece than we are at home—but who cares. Worth it.

As soon as we pull up outside of the airport, I

race inside, eyes pinned to the departures board. I scan for the flight number Greg gave me—he booked her flight with his own miles, last minute, since he thought he was doing the right thing. Helping her out, freeing her from a situation that was upsetting her.

I don't blame him—well, except for the being such a jerk to her when she first met my parents part. But even then, he thought he was following my orders. He's been trying to help, even if he's been butchering it all the while.

My eyes find her flight number, and my heart sinks in my chest.

Departed.

No.

I whip out my phone and stare at my texts to her. There's no way to tell if she got them in time. No way to know if she'll spend her whole flight home just as depressed and down as she's been feeling tonight. I just pray she'll pick up when I call her again in the morning.

Maybe I should leave the reunion early too, catch an early flight tomorrow morning and try to meet her back home. We do this reunion every five years. I'll be back. But this may be my only chance to make things right with Dee

"Hey," says a soft voice behind me. And suddenly, I can breathe again. My chest swells, and I whip around, to find Dee, that crazy enormous pink suitcase of hers in hand, smiling tentatively at me from next to the exit doors.

CHAPTER SIXTEEN

Dee

"You didn't leave." That's the first thing he says, and he looks like I've just handed him the best Christmas present in the world by being here.

That, more than anything, reassures me that I made the right call. "It didn't feel right," I say, shuffling my feet. "Storming off like that without giving you a chance to explain… I was emotional, and hurt, and I just wanted to get out of there before more of your family members started to hate me."

He barks out a laugh, then shakes his head. "Nobody hates you, Dee."

I snort and roll my eyes. "Okay, maybe not *hate*, but certainly *dislike*."

"I just got done talking to my father, actually," Jasper says. "He said that as long as you make me happy, he's a hundred and ten percent on board with having you around. He says you're refreshing, actually, I think was the exact word."

I laugh a little louder this time. *That* I can believe, at least.

"But I realized more than that." Jasper steps closer, and just like it always does when he's close to me, my breath hitches in my throat. It's suddenly hard to take a deep breath, hard to keep my head from spinning. "You make me happy, Dee. So happy, whenever I'm with you." He wraps his hands around my shoulders, and the warmth of his hands pins me

349

in place. "But not just happy." His eyes search mine, darker and more serious than I've ever seen them. "I love you, Dee," he whispers.

My heart feels like it could explode. "I love you, Jasper," I say. As the words tumble from my mouth, I realize they're true. *I love you.* I love him more than I ever realized I could. "I know I said I never fell in love before, and that's true, but this... This is the real thing." I shake my head, shocked by it.

"I know," he whispers.

And then he drops down on one knee.

My eyes go wide as saucers. Over his shoulder, I spy Greg, looking just as surprised as I am. We lock eyes, and Greg shrugs, then winks at me, and mouths *I'm sorry.*

I shake my head. It's not his fault.

I look back at Jasper, who's drawn a small box from his pocket. "Last time I did this," Jasper says, "I didn't mean it. Not really. But this time it's different. This time… it's real."

He opens the lid of the box, and my jaw drops when I see what's nestled inside.

An engagement ring. A beautiful one. But not the one I've been wearing on my finger for the last three weeks. Not the huge gaudy one the jeweler in Newholme talked us into.

A different ring. The ring that I picked out first, the gorgeous one surrounded by sapphires, which the jeweler talked us out of getting in favor of the pricier, showier one.

"Will you marry me, Dee?" Jasper whispers.

My real ring, I think. *For my real husband.*

Just like I did the last time he knelt before me, I drop onto my knees beside him and wrap both hands around his. "Of course, you idiot," I whisper, though fresh tears spilling out of my eyes. But these aren't tears of sadness. They're tears of joy.

He fumbles the ring from the box, only barely manages to slip it onto my finger before I'm grabbing his face between and pulling him into a long, deep, lip-biting, tongue-wrestling kiss. The kind of kiss you get lost in. The kind of kiss that transports you to another world, and as his hands drop down to circle my waist and pull me against him, I arch my body into his, craving more, craving all of him, wanting to be his wife, the way we've been pretending all along.

Someone nearby clears their throat, loudly, and we break apart, breathless, only to realize I'm half on top of him, right in the middle of the airport. A few passersby are looking at us, laughing. Someone snaps a photo, and I turn my head to glare at Greg, who coughs again.

"We are still in public, you know, guys."

"Who's going to begrudge me a little PDA with my wife right now?" Jasper counters, leaning in to kiss me again, shorter but sweeter this time. Then he rises, and pulls me to my feet at his side. "What do you say, future Mrs. Quint?" He squeezes my hand, wrapped in his. This engagement ring feels so much more natural on my finger, lighter and smoother than the other. I turn it to admire the way it flashes in the airport lighting. "Shall we head back now?"

I trail after him, as Greg picks up my luggage for me, and tilt my head. "I don't understand, Jasper.

When did you buy this ring? I thought we settled on the other one."

"For show," he said. "But I remembered how much you liked this one. And then, before we came here…" He pauses. Turns a little red around the ears, the way he does whenever he's embarrassed. "Well. I thought it might come in handy, sometime in the future."

I can't help it. I burst into laughter. "And you call me the hopeless romantic?"

"Maybe we're both a little bit guilty there," he murmurs.

"You think?" Greg shouts over his shoulder as he hauls my luggage toward the trunk. I catch the tail end of mutter about *"literally racing to the airport"* under his breath, and I snort softly.

But Greg does stop us once we're in the car, and catch both our eyes where we're curled up side-by-side in the backseat. "Seriously, though, I'm sorry for all this. I thought I was doing what you wanted, Jasper—"

"It's okay," he interrupts. "You didn't know. But there is one thing you can do to make up for it..." He flashes me a look. Whispers in my ear. My eyes light up, and that's all the response he needs. "We need you to help us plan something, Greg."

****

"I don't understand." Jasper's mother looks from me to him and back again, confusion written all over her face. We're standing in the little side room

355

off the breakfast room at the resort. First thing in the morning, after driving back from the airport, we asked the Quints to meet us here to explain ourselves. Or at least, some of the story. "You're *not* married?"

"Not yet, no." Jasper runs a hand through his hair. "We... well, it's a long story. But the short version is, we were trying married life out, and it turns out, we actually really like it. And want to make a real go of it."

"And then we thought, since I don't have any family to invite, really," I speak up.

"And since our whole family is here right now..." Jasper continues.

"At this incredibly beautiful resort in a gorgeous town in Greece, which, I mean." I laugh. "I never thought I'd find myself at, let alone with so many wonderful people…"

"We just thought this would be the perfect time to seal the deal," Jasper finishes. "For real this time." At that, he glances in my direction, and winks. By the time he finishes speaking, his mother is wiping at the corners of her eyes, overcome with emotion.

"I know we might've gotten off on the wrong foot," I start to say. But I never finish the sentence, because his mother throws her arms around me to squeeze me into the tightest hug of my life.

"Not at all. We were the ones being judgmental. I hope you can forgive us." Mrs. Quint— Kara, I remind myself—steps back and glances over my head, at that. I turn to see Jasper's father smiling at us all. He'd let his wife take the lead so far, while we explained that we never legally married. Now, he crosses the room to grip Jasper's hand, then pulls him into a back-slapping hug next.

"I'm proud of you, son," he says. Then Mr. Quint—Antoine, I'm going to need to practice this— turns to hug me next. "And I'm so excited to welcome you into our family, Dee."

"Oh, goodness." Kara starts, grabbing my arms to spin me around. "What are we going to do for an outfit, though? I don't know if I have anything white that would be your size…"

That's when another voice pipes up, from a little side nook off the main room that I didn't even notice earlier. "I've got the perfect thing." Jasper's cousin Sofia pokes her head around the corner. She has a half-finished breakfast plate in her lap and an apologetic look on her face.

358

"I woke up early. Wanted to sneak away for breakfast before the kids got up. Sorry, I didn't mean to spy, but you all sort of just flooded the room before I could warn you I was here…"

Jasper laughs. "It's fine, Sofia."

Sofia extends a hand to me. "I never thought I'd get a chance to use this dress. It doesn't fit me, now I'm starting to show, but… well, come and take a look, Dee."

The next day is a whirlwind. Word slowly makes its way through the armada of cousins, and together, Jasper's family pulls together everything almost as smoothly as though this had been the plan the entire time. I know it's a whirlwind, but somehow, after wearing his engagement ring practically since the day we met—first the fake one and now the real one

—and after calling him my husband for days, it doesn't feel rushed or hurried to be getting married to him now.

It feels like it has been inevitable all along. Like somehow, deep down, from the moment we first met, this was always going to turn into the real deal.

And having Jasper's entire extended family in town for it only makes it more perfect.

The resort is accommodating, too. Originally the fourth night we were here was supposed to be a big family dinner, for which Jasper's father rented the ballroom banquet hall in the resort.

Now, however, when that fourth night arrives, I peer through a crack in the door into a room transformed. Jasper's little cousins, Sofia's kids and Chloe's twins, helped tie together bouquets of flowers, which dangle from wall sconces and decorate the backs of the chairs Jasper's uncles lined up in neat, orderly rows. With the chandeliers lit, and candles all around the front of the room, where the hotel helped set up a little dais with an archway above it, the place looks like the kind of wedding hall you'd plan for months to get perfect.

Instead, in what seems to be our luck, we just stumbled into it by accident.

I turn back around for one last double-check with Sofia.

"You look stunning," she tells me, smiling wide. She's in a jaunty little green summer dress, ruched and lovely on her. She'll stand next to me at the altar, as my maid of honor, and Jasper's father will be his best man.

"Thank you again for the loan," I say, taking another spin in her gown. It's a beautiful white off-the-shoulder dress, knee length and made from silk that feels amazing against my skin. It could pass for a cocktail gown dress in summer, but on me now, paired with the bright blue heels we borrowed from another cousin and with a veil one of Jasper's aunts dug out of her suitcase pinned into my hair, it looks like exactly the type of wedding gown I would have chosen for myself. Subtle, not too over-the-top, but beautiful in an understated way.

"Of course. But actually..." Sofia smiles at me. "I shouldn't be the one walking with you right now."

A frown-line appears between my brows. "What do you mean?"

"Jasper sent one last little surprise…" Sofia steps aside, crosses to the far end of the little alcove where I'm waiting, and sticks her head around the corner. "Come on in."

Melissa steps into the room, a huge, ear-splitting grin on her face, dressed in a gorgeous blue dress that compliments my dress perfectly.

"Holy shit!" My jaw drops. Before I can even properly react, she's launched herself across the room and wrapped her arms around me tight. "How did… how'd you even…?"

"Jasper found me on your Facebook page," she admits into my shoulder. "He noticed we're listed as sisters on there."

I laugh into her hair. An old joke, that sibling listing, which we put up years ago. Because Melissa's my only real family left, and always has been. "But…"

"He emailed me last night. Explained everything. Offered to book me a flight here, all expenses paid. How could I say no to Greece?" She smirks up at me. "Oh, and I guess my best friend's wedding, that too."

I laugh and hug her again. "I can't believe him."

"You've got a real keeper, Dee." She squeezes my shoulder. "I'm so happy for you. You ready to do this thing for real?"

I glance from Melissa to Sofia, beaming. "Ready as I'll ever be." The three of us turn together to face the aisle before us.

Through the gap in the door, I can see the whole family assembled. And there, at the head of the dais, waiting for me beside his cousin Alexander, who it turns out has one of those online minister degrees we'd joked about in our fake wedding ceremony, is Jasper. He's wearing a tux and black tie, and with his hair falling across one eye, the way it always does, and his beard freshly shaved, he looks like he could be modeling for *GQ* right now.

Is that really the man I'm about to marry? Part of me has to resist the urge to pinch myself and make sure I'm not dreaming.

"Go get him, girl," Melissa murmurs, right before she and Sofia open the doors to stride up the aisle before me.

Right on cue. Somewhere in the distance, Jasper's aunt Alyssa strikes a cord on the piano. A song I recognize begins to play, and I have to smile to myself at the choice. Jasper picked a song we listened to on our first getaway in Newholme, at a little beachside cafe with a string quartet playing for coins out on the boardwalk outside.

To that, I walk through the double doors and into the next chapter of my life.

CHAPTER SEVENTEEN

Jasper

I hold Dee in my arms and spin her across the floor. With the makeshift wedding room we put together now cleared away into dance floors and buffet tables, we have plenty of space to move. I spin her through the air, away from me and then back again, catching her in my arms and dipping her backward over my arm a little.

Her eyes flash when I pull her upright again, and I'm struck all over at how lucky I am. How impossibly perfect Dee is.

"Are you enjoying yourself, Mrs. Quint?" I

murmur as I pull her flush against me for the tail end of our first dance. The music fades out, a new song strikes up, and my cousins, aunts and uncles flood the dance floor in pairs and gaggles.

"More than you could possibly know, Mr. Quint," she whispers against my ear. The whisper of her lips against my skin drives me wild. All I can think about is tonight, what I plan to do to her once I get her back to our suite, all alone in my arms.

My wife.

A few days ago I was already calling her that, and it sounded so right, despite the fact that it was all a sham. Now... Now it just feels natural. Normal.

Perfect.

"I don't know about that," I murmur in response, pausing to nip playfully at the soft spot on her neck just below her ear. I savor the faint sigh of desire she makes. "I think I have a pretty good idea how enjoyable this whole day has been. And every day, in fact, since the day I first met you."

She turns her gorgeous smile on me then, and I can honestly say I have never been happier in my entire life.

We eat, drink and dance the night away with my family. We listen to my father's embarrassing toast about how he can't wait for the grandkids. Melissa, Dee's best friend, who I mistook for her sister online, but who's turned out to be an even more perfect addition to this wedding, delivers an equally embarrassing toast about Dee's exploits. Dee dabs her teary eyes through my mother's toast about how overwhelmed with gratitude she is about being able to witness our special day and be here with us for it.

Sofia cracks us all up with story after story of the crazy shit I did when we were growing up together. Then Alex starts in on more embarrassing details about my childhood, and I finally have to intervene and save the day.

"Dee," I say, when I take the microphone from—well, more like wrestle it off of—Alex. "When I first met you, I knew there was something different about you. Something remarkable." I hold her gaze, hope she hears the note of humility in my tone. I do still feel bad about what made us pull her file out of the pile, what made Greg recommend her to me. But not that bad, because if Greg hadn't picked Dee to be my fake wife, we wouldn't be here today. I'd never have met her, never have gotten to know her vivacious personality and everything else that makes her impossible to forget.

"Every day since then," I continue, "you've proven to me, over and over, that I was right that first day. You're the perfect match for me. The perfect wife. And I promise you now, I will strive to be the perfect husband for you, in turn, in all the days left to come. Thank you for shaking up my life, Dee." I flash her a secret little smile. "And for forcing me out of my abject bachelorhood."

Laughter fills the room.

"I love you, and I wouldn't have this any other way."

I love you, Dee mouths back, and my heart could burst.

****

"Finally alone together, Mrs. Quint." I tighten my arms around her. Run them along her curves, exploring her skin through the silky fabric of her dress. "Now, I think it's time to take advantage of my husbandly duties for the first time."

She grins up at me, eyebrows raised. "Is that so, Mr. Quint?"

"Oh, yes."

We're on the balcony outside our suite. The rest of the resort is dark, lights out, most people passed out asleep, stuffed full of food from the buffet and drinks from the open bar tab we kept running late into the night. Somewhere far down below, in the gardens on the first floor, I see a pinprick of light, catch distant strains of voices, too far away to make out, from the aunts and uncles still up late gossiping.

But up here, on the terrace, it's just the two of us and the moon overhead, full and bright, shining down and illuminating Dee's skin and eyes so she looks otherworldly.

She shifts against me, and I feel every inch of her body against mine like a shot of adrenaline in my veins. My cock jumps against my zipper, strains toward her. I tuck her hair behind her ears, cup her chin in both hands and tilt her face up toward mine, claiming her mouth with mine, savoring the feel of her velvety soft lips parting under mine, the twine of her tongue through mine.

She turns back toward the room, but I stop her with one hand, a smile tugging at the edges of my mouth.

She draws back from the kiss, and her eyebrows rise. "Out here?" she whispers.

I glance around us, pointedly. Aside from the lights far down in the garden, not visible unless you lean over the edge of the terrace, there's nobody else awake. And no one down there could see us up here either. "Why not?"

Her cheeks flush in the moonlight. "I married a dirty man, didn't I, Mr. Quint?"

"My wife has a dirty mind herself," I counter, stepping toward her and reaching down to catch the hem of her gown. I lift it up slowly, teasing, enjoying the sight of her skin being revealed inch by inch in the moonlight. The warm breeze hugs us from all sides, but I still notice goosebumps rise on the edge of her neck when I draw the dress completely off, and she stands before me in a lacy little bra and thong set, a sexy barely-there lingerie outfit like I've never seen on her before.

If I was hard before, that's nothing compared to the pulse of white hot desire I feel go straight to my cock now.

"You like it?" Dee turns, and the sight of her tight ass in the thong makes me want to bend her over the railing right now and take her. But I plan to take tonight slow. I plan to enjoy every inch of my brand new wife.

My wife. Just the thought makes this hotter— knowing she's mine, we belong to one another.

"I love it," I reply. "But I'd like it on the floor better." I smirk. She reaches to hook a thumb under the thong, but I stop her. "Not yet." I tilt my head. Undo my tie first, and toss that back into the room, before I start to undo the buttons on my tuxedo shirt.

It takes me no time at all to strip down, and when I pull off my boxers, Dee's gaze goes straight to my cock, her tongue wetting her lips like she can already taste me—like she's as hungry for me as I am for her. "I want to feel your cock inside me, husband," she murmurs, and the sound of those words make me tense even more. "No condoms tonight." She raises her eyes to mine.

"I agree." I step toward her, eyes locked. Closer and closer until the tip of my cock presses against the soft, velvet-smooth skin of her belly. She reaches up to cup me between her hands. "I want to take you raw. I want to come inside you, wife."

She shivers with delight, and strokes her hands along me, gaze locked to mine. "I want you to put a baby in me, husband," she whispers.

Only then do I hook my fingers under her panties. Slowly ease the thong down her legs, and kick it aside. She steps toward me, but I grab her hips and spin her around. Bend her forward, so her chest touches the wide railing on our balcony. I spread her legs and position myself behind her, both of us looking out over the amazing view. But me, I have eyes only for the view right beneath me. My wife, looking sexy as fucking hell when she turns around to gaze up at me over her shoulder, her lower lip caught between her teeth in a taunting, teasing smirk.

"You want to take me right here, husband?" she asks, voice low. "In front of God and the whole world?"

"Fuck yes I do." I slide my hand between her legs, pausing to cup her ass, massage it between my firm fingers. Then I slide those fingers down to her slit, slipping between her lips to run my middle finger through her slick juices. She's already soaked for me, and she only gets wetter as I begin to stroke my finger along her, coating my finger in her juices, making her so wet that a trickle runs down her inner thigh before I finally position my cock behind her, raw like we said.

I trace my tip along her slit now, collecting her juices, coating the tip of my fat cock in them. "Do you want me to claim you, wife? Do you want me to make you mine once and for all?"

"Fuck yes," she gasps, her voice hissed through her clenched teeth. "Take me, Jasper. Fuck me, right here."

I press into her slow, an inch at a time. She twists against me, pushing her hips back to try to speed me up. But I pin her in place with one hand, and reach around with my other to tease her breasts, drawing one from the confines of her lacy bra to massage with my hand. She moans and arches her back forward toward the sensation, and I roll her hardening nipple between two fingers, pinching her just hard enough to let her feel it, not enough to hurt.

"God your pussy is so fucking perfect, Dee. Have I ever told you that?"

She bucks back against me, but I tighten my grip on her waist, hold her there, bent over the railing, and take my time stroking in and out of her. Long, slow strokes so she can adjust to my girth, feel the full length of my cock as I stretch and plunge into her pussy. "You… might have… mentioned," she manages to pant.

Her moans grow longer, lower, throatier, as I start to move a little faster, thrusting into her now, both of our bodies rocking with the motion. She lifts her tight little ass toward me, and I pause caressing her breasts to lightly swat her ass, just hard enough to make her gasp and buck in surprise, not enough to hurt.

She flashes me a coy smile and reaches back to grab my ass, pull me forward into her again.

Eventually I build up to a rhythm, fucking her hard from behind, loving the sight of her tits bouncing below her and her eyes, still on mine with her head half-turned toward me, hooded with pleasure.

"You like that, wife? You like feeling my thick raw cock in your pussy?"

I slide one hand down the plane of her stomach, until I reach the mound of her pussy. If I hold my hand there, I can feel the pressure from my cock thrusting in and out of her, stuffing her full all the way to her belly. Then I circle my fingers around the edges of her clit, moving closer and closer to it in concentric circles.

"Fuck... Jasper... I'm going to come, fuck. Don't stop."

Before long she cries aloud, unable to stifle the sound, and gasps, her pussy convulsing around my cock, gripping me like a fist when she comes. But I can tell from the way she glances around us that she's worried someone will have heard that. So before I near my own climax, I pull out of her.

She lets out a little mewl of protest, but I just reach down and flip her up into my arms and carry her back across the threshold. "Enough sharing you with the whole world tonight," I say, my voice a low growl. "You're all mine now, wife."

Back inside our suite, we collide with the wall, and I wrap her legs around my waist. She tightens them around me and grips my shoulders to hold herself up, while I position my cock against her entrance again. I hold her there, pinned against the wall as I thrust in and out of her, fast thrusts that grow faster as the pressure starts to build at the base of my cock. "Come again for me, wife," I say, tilting her head to kiss her neck, her shoulder, the spot where they meet. "Come for me, Dee."

Her breath speeds up as I continue to fuck her. I angle her against the wall so my cock curves up against her inner walls, stroking over her G-spot, my tip dragging against that little sensitive spot until her breaths become pants and moans of desire. "I'm so close, Jasper. Don't stop."

"Tell me you're mine, Dee."

"I'm yours. Fuck. I'm yours," she says, the second time louder, nearly a shout, a cry, as she rushes over the edge into another orgasm, stronger than the last. Her legs tense around me, and her toes curl, her fingernails digging into the bare skin of my shoulder as the orgasm races through her.

I'm not far behind. I fuck her with abandon now, those words *I'm yours* too hot coming from her, too impossibly sexy for me to stop now even if I wanted to. And I don't want to stop.

I don't ever want to stop pleasuring Dee.

"You want a baby?" I ask her, tone low.

"Yes," she moans, breathy. "Give me a baby, Jasper. Put a baby in me."

"I'll put a baby in your belly. I'm going to fill you with my cum, Dee." I thrust faster, harder. Grip her ass and lift her up against me, arching up with one last hard thrust. I feel my cock hit home within her, sliding all the way in to the hilt, as the orgasm hits. I shoot rush after rush of hot cum into her, filling her with my seed. She cries aloud, almost as loud as when she came herself, and buries her face in my neck, breathing hard.

"Fuck," she whispers, when she finally has the

384

strength to unhook her legs from mine and stand again, albeit on shaky legs. I hold her up, and when I draw my cock out of her pussy, a hot rush of our mingled juices spills down her inner thigh, trickles all the way to the floor.

I grin and drop to my knees. Pull her hips to my face and, unable to help myself, lean in to kiss her mound. Her clit. I flick my tongue against her, over her hot pussy, red from the pounding it just took. I lick her and suck her, tasting our juices mingled in her sweet pussy, and then I flick my tongue over her clit, again and again, until her head falls back against the wall and she lets out a wail of pleasure, echoing in the high-ceilinged room.

I will never tire of making my wife cry out in pleasure like that. I'll never get tired of Dee, period.

I love her, now and forever.

CHAPTER EIGHTEEN

Dee

We speed along the test track. Well. I speed along, and Jasper whoops in appreciation from the passenger side seat. It's my turn to take our latest model out for a spin—one that I helped design. I worked my way up into the design element of the internship all on my own, I might add, with no special recommendations from the boss. Aside from the stellar letter of recommendation Greg wrote me (since we figured a letter from my own husband would look a little strange on an application), which landed me a position in a top university right here in town.

Not only will I be able to keep interning at Quint Motors, but I'll finally be able to start pursuing the degree that will grant me the qualifications to work here full-time as soon as I graduate.

Who says you can't mix business and pleasure?

Right now, it feels like the two are pretty in sync, as I floor the gas and whip toward the corner of the track.

"Careful at this part," Jasper warns me, but it's habit—we've been through this so many times, in so many models of cars. He knows I can handle myself behind the wheel at this point. We both can.

Still, I take extra care, today of all days, when I round the corner. I've got some surprises up my sleeve for my husband today, after all.

It's been six months since our whirlwind wedding. Since we returned from the trip on which we were supposed to pretend to be husband and wife as actual husband and wife. And since that day, my love for Jasper has only grown, every single moment we spend together. He's every bit the supportive husband I could ask for, and my biggest cheerleader. Not to mention his family has adopted me as one of their own, taking it upon themselves to include me in more family group chats than I can handle, and inviting me to every family event and gathering they've had since their big Greece reunion—the one that turned into our surprise wedding celebration halfway through.

The one thing we haven't gotten yet, however,

is the start to a family of our own. We've been trying, ever since our wedding night, but sometimes these things take time.

"There's no rush," Jasper is always reminding me. "We have the rest of our lives for this." But I notice the way he watches his little cousins, the longing expression he gets in his eye whenever he holds Sofia's youngest in his arms. She's only a few months old now, and cute as can be. Getting to the fussy stage, but at least for now we can pass her back.

Pretty soon, we won't be able to do that. But the funny thing is, I'm more than excited enough for that moment to arrive.

We speed around the corner of the test track, and I head for another loop. That's when Jasper notices. "Hey, where are the pit crew?" he asks.

"I gave them an early lunch. Told them not to bother us the rest of the day," I say, momentarily trailing off as I maneuver through one particularly tricky part of the track.

When I'm back on a straightaway, I turn to see my husband watching me with a tilt to his head, suspicion dawning in his eyes. "Why did you do that?"

I grin, mischief flooding my face. I can never keep a secret from Jasper for long, damn him. "I figured we could have some fun," I say, to cover up the whole story. In reality, my whole body is already buzzing with excitement at what's going to happen today. How everything will change.

"Oh really." Jasper's voice drops low and suggestive. "What sort of… fun?"

"Well. You and I both love cars," I point out.

"We did establish that day one." He smirks.

I shift gears and speed off the side of the track toward the pull-off. I skid to a halt there and then throw the car in park. There's nobody else in the test track room—I cordoned the whole thing off. Blocked it in the calendar as reserved for a private testing event, and sent the rest of the staff home early. It's just us here. Me, Jasper, and the sexy new car I helped his team design.

"And yet, we've never fooled around in one," I say, head tilted in mock shock. "I wonder why that is."

"Fooled around?" He smirks. "What are we, teenagers?"

"Okay." I lock eyes with him. Start to climb over into the passenger side seat. "We've never fucked in a car, Jasper. Much less a car I helped design. A car your company produced and built. A car I just tore through this test track driving. Don't you think we're missing out on a golden opportunity?"

By the time I reach his side of the car and straddle his lap, I can tell he agrees by the thick bulge in his jeans, pressing through his pants and against my crotch.

He reaches down for the pencil skirt I'm wearing. "Hmm, you make some excellent points there, Mrs. Quint. I think we need to see what we can do about rectifying this situation." With that, he pushes the skirt up around my waist…

Only to find I'm not wearing anything beneath.

His eyebrows shoot up, and his mouth curls in

pleasure. "Did you go all day without panties, Mrs. Quint?"

I catch his eye, lift one brow. "I did indeed, Mr. Quint."

"You're a dirty girl." He grabs my waist and pulls me down on top of him, the press of his cock digging against my bare pussy through his pants. Then he reaches between my legs, making sure to graze my clit with his thumb along the way, and undoes the zipper of his pants.

"I'm *your* dirty girl," I clarify, leaning in to trail my tongue up the side of his neck. "And today I don't want to just drive this car. I want to take my husband for a test drive too."

He pulls out his thick cock, and just like every time I see it, I inhale, sharp, my belly tensing with want. *He's so big.* I love looking at him, feeling him.

I reach down to catch him, stroking his velvety length with both hands so I can cup him tight enough to make him suck in that sharp little breath between his teeth, the way I love making him do… But he catches my wrists and pulls them back. Pins them behind me in one hand, so I'm straddling him with my hands behind my back.

"You know what I like best about having you on top of me?" Jasper asks. With his other hand, he pushes my shirt up. Frees my breasts from my bra, one after the other, and leans in to bite and suck at my nipples until I cry out faintly, both nipples hard at his touch. Then he pulls me back again, and reaches down to grip his cock instead. "I love watching you ride my fat cock."

He positions me over his tip, and eases me down against him, until the spongy tip of his cock spreads my pussy lips and pauses at my entrance, poised there, waiting. He circles his cock against me, teasing. I can feel myself getting wetter, and my clit positively throbs with desire.

"Let me ride you, Jasper."

"Not yet." He arches a brow. "First, I want to know what we're really doing here."

I suck in another breath. Damn. He knows me too well. "What do you mean?" I try to keep my voice light, even. "I wanted to fuck you out here, Jasper."

"I know." He grins, a dark, playful slash. "And I'll fuck you, Dee. But first, you tell me what else you're hiding. You didn't tell all the employees to go home just for this, did you? Because…" He reaches down to stroke my clit with one thumb, slow and circular, the motion driving me wild.

I buck against him, but he's still holding my hands behind my back, both my wrists in one of his hands, making it impossible for me to go far.

"That would be very naughty indeed, wife." Then, without warning, he stops. Stops stroking my clit, and eases away from me so the tip of his cock isn't pressed against my entrance anymore.

"Okay," I pant, capitulating. "Okay, I wanted to surprise you, after the hooking up… But…" His thumb glides back to my clit and I let out a faint little groan of pleasure. "But I'll show you now." I twist one hand in his, and arch a brow. He releases me, and I sit up, just far enough to reach behind me to the glove compartment. I pop it, and withdraw the gift-wrapped, slender box I hid in there.

"For you, husband." I pass it to him with a grin.

He arches a brow at me, clearly confused. Then he undoes the ribbon around the package, and peels it open. Inside is a simple white stick. But that stick makes his eyebrows shoot up and his jaw drop. "Is this...?" He picks it up. Turns it over.

On the other side of the stick is a little red plus sign. "Oh my God," he whispers.

"Congratulations, Daddy," I murmur, positively beaming now.

Jasper lets out a shout of joy, then grabs me and pulls me down into a hard kiss. When we break apart again, happiness shines from his eyes. "Dee, oh my God. We're going to have a baby."

"We're going to have a baby," I agree, and kiss him again, and again. I lose track of myself in his mouth, his lips, his tongue tracing the edges of mine, familiar and invigorating all at once.

This time, when he pulls me back across his hips, he doesn't tease me. He glides right into me, his cock stretching and filling my pussy, making me gasp aloud at the sensation of feeling *whole*. A feeling I get whenever I'm with him, and especially when he's inside me, completing me like this. I wrap my arms around his shoulders and rock against him, savoring the thickness and length of him, the heat of his mouth where he kisses my neck, my jawline, my collarbone. His tongue flicks across my clavicle, traces the edges of my neck, and he nips along my ear gently, just hard enough to make me gasp and twist in his arms.

Finally, when he's had enough of teasing me, he grips my hips in his strong hands and holds me in place over his body. He thrusts up into me, fucking me hard, and I rock down against him, riding him for all I'm worth. I glance down between us to watch the sight of his thick cock plunging into my pussy. That's when he lifts a hand to my belly. Holds it there against me as he continues to thrust up into me, and I press my hand down over his, eyes half shut with pleasure and joy and all the other conflicting emotions rioting through me at once.

We come at the same time, both of our cries sharp in the tight car, and I collapse across him, the windows around us fogged by now, blocking us even farther from anyone's sight beyond. He leans the seat back, and I lie along him, savoring the sweet ache between my legs, the fullness of feeling in my belly, and the way our breath mingles, our chests rising and falling in sync as he holds me in his arms, protective and nurturing all at once.

"I can't believe it," he finally whispers, after a long moment of silence, and he reaches down to kiss the top of my head, his lips lingering against my hair for a moment.

"You're going to be a father," I whisper back, leaning up to catch his eye and smile. "And a fucking great one at that, if your own father is anyone to judge by." I allow for a wry smile. "The insistence on his need for grandchildren aside."

Jasper laughs, his chest vibrating pleasantly

underneath me with the sound of it. "And you're going to be the best mother around, Dee. I just know it." His arms slip down to my waist. He kisses my forehead, my cheeks, one after the other, then the tip of my nose. Then my lips, soft and sweet. "I can't wait to meet our little race car driver."

I snort out a laugh. "Um, our little race car *designer*, thank you very much. She'll take after me in the career department."

"She? You don't think he'll be the next speed devil in a long line of his father" speed demon family?"

We both grin and shake our heads. "Either way," I say.

"I can't wait to see what the future brings," Jasper whispers. "And I'm so lucky that I have you in my life, to face that future with."

We're silent for another long moment, then distracted by more kisses, our hands trailing over one another's bodies. Jasper flips me over beneath him, and his hands wander down my hips, before he pauses, a laugh catching him by surprise.

I tilt my head and arch one brow. "What's so funny?"

"I was just thinking. If it's a boy, maybe we ought to name him after the person responsible for getting us together in the first place."

I snort. But I don't hate the idea, either. "Baby Greg?" I arch one brow. "He'd probably hate us for it."

"He'd claim to, but deep down I think he'd secretly love it." Jasper laughs. "I do have a lot to

403

thank him for, at the end of the day." Jasper cups my cheek and turns my face toward his. Then he tucks back a stray hair from my forehead. "I have him to thank for my entire life, now, Dee. Because you... you're not just my wife. You're my whole world."

"And you're mine," I whisper. Together, we fall back into the kiss. This time, when Jasper begins to harden against my thigh, I spread my legs wide and wrap them around his waist. Let him lie down along me, as we get to work steaming up the windows of this car again.

In this moment, I realize... I couldn't ask for anything else in life. I have everything I've ever dreamed of and more.

THE END

Author Biography

Penny Wylder writes just that-- wild romances. Happily Ever Afters are always better when they're a little dirty, so if you're looking for a page turner that will make you feel naughty in all the right places, jump right in and leave your panties at the door!

Other Books by Penny Wylder

Filthy Boss

Her Dad's Friend

Rockstars F#*k Harder

The Virgin Intern

Her Dirty Professor

The Pool Boy

Get Me Off

Caught Together

The Billionaire's Gamble

Seven Days With Her Boss

Virgin in the Middle

The Virgin Promise

First and Last

Tease

Spread

Bang

Second Chance Stepbrother

Dirty Promise

Sext

Quickie

Bed Shaker

Deep in You

The Billionaire's Toy

Buying the Bride

Dating My Friend's Daughter

Perfect Boss

The Roommate's Baby

Cowboy Husband

FLIRT

LUST

CLAIM

Made in the USA
San Bernardino, CA
30 March 2019